Blood, Sex & Violence

A VAMPIRE'S REBUTTAL

emil jersey

TRIGGER WARNINGS

1. NON-EXPLICIT depiction; Rakum have consensual sex as children.
2. This novel contains NON-EXPLICIT depictions of gay, bi, and straight sexual relationships.
3. Contains occasional references to a Creator.

Blood Sex and Violence A Vampire's Rebuttal
By Emil Jersey
First Edition, ©2019 by Emil Jersey

Rated for Mature Teen & Adult / Language, Violence & non-explicit Sexual Situations.
Explicit Warning – NONE

ISBN-13: 978-0-9960505-1-7
Also available in eBook

Run Rabbit Books
A Division of Little Roni Publishers, LLC
www.littleronipublishers.com/run-rabbit-books.php

Cover Image © Gleb TV at 123rf.com, Licensed.
Photos of Jersey, Hester, Win, and Stone, used by License, 123rf.com

Send inquiries regarding this rebuttal to:
submissionsLRP@gmail.com
Subject Line: BSV

www.EmilJersey.com

PUBLISHED IN THE UNITED STATES OF AMERICA

I GO BY JERSEY.

THE BOOK IN YOUR HAND IS THE UNRATED VERSION.
I do not like being censored.

I AM A RAKUM,
a powerful, ancient, godlike race descended from angels.

WHY A REBUTTAL? Beth Rider's novel[1] indicates my people are involved in an epic spiritual war outside of our awareness. I am not a puppet. None of us are. I aim to reveal what she does not have the balls to discuss. I have balls.

Read on and you will understand how she missed the best part about being a god.

~ *Jersey*

---

[1] Beth Rider told her story in a bestselling vampire novel entitled, *Rabbit: Chasing Beth Rider* (writing as Ellen C. Maze). To learn more about her experience among my brethren, visit www.ellencmaze.com. ~ Jersey

REGARDING MY PEOPLE

Rakum (RAH′-kum) a.k.a Wraith, from Heb. raca; "vain thing."
Def: From Semitic mythology; a race of vampire-like beings,
thought to be descended from fallen angels.

THIS REBUTTAL IS ABOUT SEX

The Fix-it Man ~ an expert in pleasure.
Each Rakum youth discovers his key strength(s) by age eight.
From there, it is up to the group lair proctors to develop and hone
these natural propensities until age thirteen when he is assigned an
Elder who initiates First Ritual, a training process lasting up to ten
years. In any generation, less than one in a thousand are discovered
to be *ish-mikhan* (also called, "fix-it men"), **Rakum born
with the propensity to sexually service Elders.**

THE ISH-MIKHAN

Jersey
Darcy Vandiver
Hester (a.k.a. asshole)

Table of Contents

IF YOU READ BETH RIDER'S NOVEL SERIES FIRST, *understand that my rebuttal was written before the event we call, "11/13," when all my brethren transformed into mortals. A wholly sucky date, to be sure, but let's focus on the positive.* ~ *Jersey*

Preface
The Rebuttal is Also My Memoir

My name is Jersey, born in 1699. In 2012, thousands of my brethren turned mortal—I did NOT. This is my memoir of my long life at the top of the food chain and the treasure of all my Elders.

You should know: We are vampires. Our race is called, "Rakum" (RAH′-kum), discussed at length in *The Rabbit Saga* 5-novel series by Ellen C. Maze.

But that author left me out until Book Five. I think you'll understand why once you get started. For starters, I don't like to be censored…

This rebuttal is about sex. I'm what we call, *ish-mikhan*, a "fix-it man," an expert in pleasure. I was born this way and we're very rare—as you'll read—and coveted by all who meet us (which has been fun).

Let's get started. You are going to love this…

We will start at the beginning—Jersey as a boy.

Seven-Plus-Eight

Jersey Identified as Ish-Mikhan

Year 1706

Eleven Rakum proselytes populated the lair house, ranging in age from seven to thirteen, Jersey being the youngest. The low pupil residency required only a single proctor/instructor who went by the moniker, Gash. When including two resident cooks, the facility housed a total of fourteen Rakum. It was the older of the two cooks that first identified Jersey as ish-mikhan.

Jersey entered the table-room at a jog, racing his brethren for the choice meats. First come-first serve kept them fierce, and at least twice a week, he outran his lair mates. Tonight, he hit the line third and put out his tray. Instead of plopping his portion onto the pewter platter, the thick and frowning chef called Otto removed the dish from his hand, tossed it into the sink and instructed him to stand still and shut up. Jersey did so, his eyes flitting between the two tall Rakum as they discussed him, speaking over his head in Hungarian. All Rakum spoke at least four languages—English, Hungarian, Hebrew, and the Rakum dialect,[2] so Jersey followed their conversation, happy to be their focus even if he didn't yet know why.

"I am one-hundred-percent certain this one is a fix-it man," Otto said, scrutinizing Jersey with intent. Uncle, the other cook, watched him, too, slowly running his eyes across Jersey's tiny frame. He was small—even for seven-plus-eight (*seven years, eight months*). Slight and nimble as a gymnast, Proctor Gash had

---

[2] *(Our leaders say that the Rakum language is "unknowable" to mortals. So far, so good. ~Jersey)*

already guessed he'd be more an intellect than a soldier, but tonight, the cook saw beyond the everyday grunt assignment.

"Come back here," Uncle commanded.

Without hesitation, Jersey joined the adults behind the low counter. When the same Rakum gestured he wait, he did, watching them serve the remainder of the lair members. Proctor Gash had not joined them, so Jersey wondered what the two men had for him to do. He took orders from everyone on the premises and had learned well that as the youngest, he was subservient to all. When every brother was fed, the cooks escorted Jersey into the interior rooms where the wood-burning stove crackled on the far wall, filling the space with the pleasant aroma of cedar. Otto and Uncle turned to Jersey, hands on their hips.

"What's the test? He won't have a sexual thought for decades. How can anyone tell this young?" Uncle shook his head, still speaking to Otto with no regard to Jersey.

"In 1600, I tested a pre-rit[3] for *ish-mikhan*. It's not difficult." Otto waved Jersey closer and touched his cheek, cupped it, and his thumb caressed the skin under his eye. "It's not about sex—it's a reaction. It happens inside them." Otto's voice grew soft and he fell into his thoughts, his eyes deep into Jersey's. Jersey did not dare look aside. Master Gash taught them fierce concentration in all things, so although the Rakum spoke over his education level, Jersey felt certain they would soon explain.

"Okay, do it," Uncle said just as softly, moving to Otto's side to face Jersey head-on. "Test him…"

"I will," Otto mumbled and dropped the contact with Jersey's face. Maintaining the eye-lock, he unbuckled his trousers. "Pup, clear your mind."

Jersey did as instructed; Gash had taught them to envision a blank white wall. All adult Rakum were telepathic and Otto humphed with approval at Jersey's mental acuity. He grasped the

---

[3] Pre-Ritual student; all Rakum go through the brutal trials of First Ritual from age 13 to 20 before they are considered mature.

waistband of his stiff woolen pants.

"Now, act on instinct. Do not think. *Act.*" Otto said the last word telepathically and his pants dropped to his ankles.

Jersey considered the cook's genitals. He'd seen them before, as all those in the lair bathed, ate, and slept, communally. Now, he was supposed to *do* something. What should he do? What action would bring the most favor upon the smallest Rakum in the lair? Jersey set his jaw; he wasn't supposed to think. Relaxing his mind, Jersey reached forward and wrapped his hand around the cook's penis. A sound of surprise came from Uncle, and Otto remained quiet. Jersey studied the white wall of his mind and allowed the outer world to muffle. The light of the oil lamps diffused into a brownish gold, the hum of his brothers chittering on a dozen topics in the next room became an incoherent buzz, slowly also disappearing into his subconscious. The one sensation indwelling Jersey's innerspace that multiplied as his five senses faded blossomed with a rosy-gold hue, and a bubbling contentment filled his being. Jersey watched the edges of the phenomenon creep, fanning outward, erasing everything tangible and satisfying his psyche to the utmost. Jersey licked his lips; the glow was alive, and it petted him singing his praises. By the time it developed a voice of its own, singing a new song of worship, telling of his magnificence, gentle fingers squeezed the back of his neck.

"Jersey?" The tender grip wiggled with a smidge more weight. "Pup? Wake up." Jersey looked upward and to his left. Master Gash stood over him and Jersey found he was standing, his palm flat against the cook's naked hip. He swallowed, grinned, and tucked his hands into his pockets.

"Masters," he said and took time to meet each of the three adult Rakum's eyes. "I'm *ish-mikhan.*" Jersey hadn't planned to say those words, but he allowed the rosy glow of his memory to speak in his stead. He must have said something wonderful because all three masters smiled and clapped first his small shoulder and then each other's. Otto readjusted his clothing, nodded to Gash, and returned to the table room. Uncle spoke with Gash over Jersey's head, reporting what he'd seen and asking questions for his own edification. When Uncle shuffled out, Gash regarded him with a grin.

"This is fantastic news, little brother," he said and turned away, walking from the room at a clip.

Jersey followed, jogging to keep up, and happy to see his master so gay. They reached Gash's personal quarters and he instructed Jersey to undress.

"Lay flat and wait." Gash leaned against the wall, crossed his arms and lowered his chin. Jersey shrugged off his loose trousers and plain white smock and made himself comfortable on the stiff straw mattress. In his peripheral vision, Gash rolled in his lips, his eyes closed and squeezing—he was calling someone telepathically and Jersey rolled his head to the side to watch. In another minute, Gash nodded and took a deep breath. He met Jersey's eye.

"We have the go-ahead from the Fathers. Tonight, right now, you will be cut—it's an honor—and in three days, the closest Elder will be by for the official identification."

"Yes, Master," Jersey said, aware that the cutting meant his foreskin would be removed. Among the Rakum, the Ten Fathers, the One Hundred Elders, and the ish-mikhan were the only ones cut in this way. Jersey resisted a grin, enjoying how he suddenly became very much like the leaders of their people.

"It's good, pup," Gash said matching his exuberance. "They say it is a wonderful existence. You will be happy."

"I am happy, Master," he said and allowed a high laugh. Gash scrunched his nose, ready to perform the light surgery. His proctor was a healer so even though Jersey's body was too young to regenerate as quickly as it would when he matured, Gash made certain he healed within minutes.

The next three sun-ups, Jersey bunked with Gash, who showed him what he could of the fix-it man's trade. He had admitted there were experts, proctors who had trained up ish-mikhan in the past, and one would come once the Elder confirmed Gash's findings. Also, there had never been an Elder in the lair, so his proctor explained how they differed.

"Elders are bred differently, raised and trained differently, treated differently by the senior Elders and Fathers," Gash explained as they lay together awaiting the moon. "The shit grunts survive makes us stronger. Elders die and are revived multiple times, learning amazing abilities we can barely fathom. They are superior. When you see your first Elder, as ish-mikhan, it may be overwhelming. Do your best to stay upright."

Jersey nodded, wondering to what extent the meeting would affect him. An hour beyond the fourth sundown from being identified, he found out.

Elder Emil rode to the lair house atop a huge Friesian stallion. Jersey had been watching from the front window and when Gash sent him a nod, he trotted for the door and swung it open as the larger-than-life Rakum reached the entrance.

"Master! Welcome!" Jersey said, his voice high and small in his own ears. When would he be big enough to sound serious and important? He fell to his knees, his hands behind his back and chin tucked into his chest, determining to corral his internal complaints.

"Oh, yes!" the Elder said, crossing the foyer with huge strides and reaching for Jersey with hands as big as pie plates. He swooped Jersey into his arms, cradled him like an infant, and looked into his face. "Beautiful and perfect!" Emil cooed, and nuzzled the hair at Jersey's forehead.

"Master honors me," Jersey said, as he'd been instructed, but inside wanting to use different words.

Elder Emil inhaled and using a measured telekinetic electric shock jolted Jersey to catch his attention. "You would have said something else?" he asked Jersey still in his arms. "Lesson

Number One: most of what a fix-it man does is instinctual. What did you *want* to say?" Emil held his gaze, fierce green-hazel eyes nearly hidden by his deep brow. Jersey swallowed and said with a small voice the words he'd first wanted to respond.

"Seeing you ride up on that magnificent beast," Jersey began and then braved on, "causes my heart to race. Let me show you, let me prove my loyalty. I am small, but something inside of me says I can make you so very proud."

Emil grinned and since he still held him like a child, he pulled Jersey to his face and kissed his mouth, first a quick peck and then longer. When he pulled back, he lowered Jersey to the ground.

"I will allow you to try," he said and indicated he'd follow if Jersey should lead him away. "You may start now."

Jersey grinned, grasped his fingers and tugged him down the hall. The lair house had guest quarters suitable for the Elder's evening visit and he brought him in there. Emil closed and bolted the door with telekinesis.

"Okay, little brother, fix me." And three months shy of eight years old, Jersey did a pretty good job.

The Elder-Candidate

Jersey Meets the Great Kilmeade

Year 1769

Elder Emil walked Jersey through First Ritual finding him to be hardy, strong, affable, and clever above and beyond his duties as the master's occasional fix-it man. Jersey was happy, life was good, and by the time he'd reached his seventieth birthday,[4] he began to develop a sexual appetite of his own and Emil never once restricted his movements. Because of that freedom, the evening the Fathers sent an Elder-Candidate to reside with them in the house, Jersey had been unprepared for the restrictions such a guest demanded.

As Jersey and his roommates waited out the sun in their light-tight bunker, they spoke in hushed tones regarding the evening ahead, all three aware none of their conversation got past Elder Emil in his quarters several rooms away.

"The master will keep you close," Justice whispered an hour before sunup. "Q overheard the preparation discussions. Oft-mentioned was the ish-mikhan's total availability."

On his opposite side, Q nodded with fervor. "What if you're transferred to the new master?" His voice arced as he abandoned the whisper. "Judas Priest! Roll over! Shit!" he said, shoving Jersey's shoulder as the three lay abreast on the blanket-covered mattress.

Jersey did not move. "You forget yourself, idiot," he said returning to their lower tones. "You're here for me, not the other way around."

---

[4] On average, the Rakum are sexually mature around the century mark.

8

Jersey had seniority over the other two only because Emil said so; both Justice and Q had seen two centuries, but as Jersey's appetite for sexual diversion grew, his master had graciously given him pick of the Elder's entourage, plus any of the Cows[5] granted access to the above-ground areas of the estate. Jersey had chosen these two Rakum based upon discerned compatibility—he hadn't known them, but with a quick read, he'd seen enough. Both Just and Q were soldiers and had served Emil since First Ritual. Jersey had served as long, but because of his *ish-mikhan* status, he'd been removed from common population before age nine. Over the past four weeks, Jersey had learned them well.

"Q has a point," Justice added and he rolled to one side to prop upon his elbow, his face to Jersey's. "Why else would you suddenly be housebound? Chained into place?"

Jersey sucked his teeth and lifted his eyes to the dark ceiling. It didn't take long to disregard the entire discussion; his master hadn't finished with him. They were deep into a new stratus of teachings and moving into more telepathic experiments. No Elder would end a project without reaching a satisfactory end. No master of Rakum would disregard the greatest pleasure of all—learning something new as a fruit of long and thoughtful labor.

Jersey shook his head, his eyes falling closed. *"Impossible,"* he sent telepathically, intentionally including his master, though his cohorts would not be aware. "My glorious master wants me close to service the new Elder—he is not done with Jersey. We have many more things to discover together."

Jersey's master petted him then, the telepathic stroke encouraging and soothing.

His two bedmates remained unconvinced. "The new Elder hails from Sicily," Q offered in a haunting timbre. "They say that Master Merlin ushered him through First Ritual, that he completed his training before age twelve."

"That is rumor, not fact," Jersey retorted. The Ritual was

---

[5] Mortals with a visceral and undeniable desire to let blood to the Rakum.

specifically designed to last from age thirteen to twenty. For a brother to complete the trials earlier did not seem possible. His body wouldn't even be mature at twelve. It was ridiculous.

Justice elbowed him hard. "He's a fucking prodigy…"

"He is an Elder at less than a hundred and forty years old," Q inserted with an edge. "Coming here is a formality—he will leave the estate fully vested. All of the brethren are abuzz with this master's unique nature and reputation."

Jersey rolled his head to meet Q's eye, deciding the men were being dramatic without cause.

Q read his expression and while one palm lifted to stroke Jersey's chest, he shook his head a tiny measure. "The brethren think Kilmeade will one day become our eleventh Father."

Jersey huffed aloud and looked back to the ceiling.

Q's hand caressed his upper body and he leaned in to press his face to Jersey's chest. He said against his skin, "Roll over, *polcz-v',*[6] we will not see you again in this way."

"You are both full of shit and I'm sick of your whining," Jersey said low, his eyes closed.

Master Emil was a mountain of power, four centuries old, the epitome of what every Rakum aspired to become—in no way could a baby Elder outdo him in any capacity. His friends were selfish, seeking one more fuck before the ish-mikhan was sequestered for an indeterminate time.

Jersey crossed his arms at his chest, the motion closing out both Justice and Q, who maneuvered to look upon his face. Jersey didn't open his eyes. "Leave me and send in Kenya," he said low. He felt no motion from the bed and he said again, more sternly. "Get the fuck out and bring Kenya. Now."

After another long moment, they rolled away and shuffled to the door. His sleeping quarters were below ground to avoid the sun and Kenya was the master's Cow and chambermaid. She was thirty, hailed from Zimbabwe, and made love like a panther.

---

[6] *Polcz-v',* favored one, an endearment only the ish-mikhan receive.

10

Jersey rose from bed, strolled to the mirror and checked his grooming. So far, the Rakum he met found him beautiful and matchless, but females were sometimes choosy. He had learned that if Kendra—or any woman—favored him, the sex was exponentially better. His long auburn hair was clean and soft, his green eyes bright—what's not to love about Jersey? Being only seventy years old, he appeared a new fifteen to mortals, but so far, the humans he invited to his bed cared not. What amused Jersey as he matured was how his mortal lovers preferred him young-looking. *All the better,* he thought, for it would be a very long time before he appeared out of his teens.

After rubbing his teeth and tongue with a rough cotton rag, Jersey fell onto the mattress and crossed his ankles to wait.

Moonrise found Jersey again making love to the chambermaid, having taken her blood after their first foray an hour ago. Elder Emil favored Jersey enough that he sent him a telepathic wake-up call, saying, *"Have another fuck with my soft brown dolly and head in. It is time."*

Kenya donned her simple dress and left as Jersey entered the small room he used as a toilet and wash area. He did not call the master's bathers, although they would have come. It was unnecessary and would only delay what Emil knew he was resisting. With game determination, Jersey sponged his body and dressed to see the master.

At Emil's chamber, the door opened wide as he entered. Elder Emil stood from a huge desk and opened his arms. He pulled Jersey close and sniffed his hair, an un-worded sentiment of, *"you have me pegged—I will never release you to an unpracticed inferior,"* echoing in his spirit. When the master's grip relaxed, Jersey looked into his face. Even before Emil opened his mouth, Jersey dreaded hearing his master dole out the new rules.

"As you are aware, the lot falls to me to graduate this youth to Elder. While he is here, you will serve him *as if he is me*. From this point forward, you must report your comings and goings. Also, I will need to spend my waking hours with him and not you; stay close, available, and invisible."

"Your will is my will," Jersey replied, and he meant it, but he didn't like sharing Emil's affection or attention. There was no time to contemplate further; before the evening ended, Elder-candidate Kilmeade waltzed into their lives.

Jersey watched him cross the great room and hid his surprise when Elder Emil dipped his head with respect. It didn't seem proper; his master had never bowed in Jersey's presence and he squirreled the information away hoping to never see such again.

There was no question the young candidate was dashing, Jersey's height and weight with wavy light-reddish brown hair that flowed in soft waves past his shoulders and reflected the light as he moved. His profile was stunning and as Jersey considered the details, Kilmeade turned his head and met Jersey's eye.

His eyes…

The Candidate's storm gray eyes shone with a zillion beams of light, invisible to the naked eye, but Jersey's ish-mikhan peculiarities caused him to see what others did not. Kilmeade smirked, his expression haughty. Jersey read a silent sentiment that translated loosely as, *"I don't need anything from you and I never will."*

Jersey revealed nothing, but inside, a battle of will began. He was jealous of the man for stealing his master's attention, he was angry at him for making Emil feel as if he needed to defer, and he was in love with him, desperate to figure out a way to make him proud. *"I will find out what he needs; we all need something,"* Jersey's mind said, and the Candidate read it all.

With a new grin, Kilmeade averted his gaze to Emil and stood akimbo. He spoke silently to Jersey's master, evident by a small eyebrow movement and then Emil gave a tiny nod.

Turning to Jersey, he said, "It is my will that you stand behind Elder-Candidate Kilmeade, literally, now, and without ceasing, until he instructs you to step off." Emil held Jersey's eye and said nothing else. Jersey realized he meant right away, and he crossed the room and positioned himself behind and square to the Candidate.

And thus, began the visit.

In total silence, Jersey walked five paces behind Kilmeade the remainder of the night and early morning, to meet all those of importance in the house, to feed on a consenting woman in the kitchen, to the toilet twice, to an otherwise private meeting with Emil and a few top soldiers, including one sent from the Ten Fathers to oversee the affair. When the sun hit the horizon, Jersey followed Kilmeade to his assigned quarters and watched Master Emil's bathers wash the young candidate head to toe. Then he followed him into his bed chamber where Kilmeade lay down, face up, giving Jersey no further instruction. Unsure exactly where to place his person, Jersey stood beside the bed, looking at the wall.

When Kilmeade fell to sleep, Jersey remained awake, reciting old lessons to himself, running over his favorite sexual escapades, and singing brothel tunes in his head.

Three hours later, Kilmeade awoke and instructed him to lie down alongside him on the narrow space. The Candidate propped onto both elbows watching Jersey with a critical eye.

"You are spoiled and precocious," he told him telepathically as Jersey positioned on his back and crossed his hands at his sternum, careful their bodies did not make contact. The Candidate continued, *"To me, you seem a wild hare, captured and in hand, but ready to bolt, unpredictable and undisciplined."*

Jersey wondered what he should respond. In his entire life, no one had ever spoken of him in a negative fashion. It felt strange, and to hear the words from a master caused a painful inner burn.

"I could tame you," Kilmeade sent and in Jersey's peripheral vision, the Candidate tilted his face to Jersey's profile. *"But I*

haven't decided if we're compatible." The Candidate sighed softly and leaned onto his back. *"It is my will that you sleep now, ish-mikhan."*

Jersey closed his eyes and his subconscious flared with a new thought—*Kilmeade wishes to taste my blood.* The Candidate chuckled softly and said nothing more. To be safe, Jersey sent the standard reply, "Whatever I have is yours." When five minutes passed with no movement and no further communication, Jersey fell to sleep.

The visit did not get better.

Every moment, Jersey walked behind or stood behind Kilmeade, and as the hours and then evenings passed, Jersey grew resentful. He still adored Emil and was compelled by his nature to adore Kilmeade, but his mischievous leanings sent him ideas of how to sew discord.

Finally, the third night of Kilmeade's stay, Jersey ran away and did not respond when his master telepathically summoned. Instead, Jersey hid in the forest. His master called him for the next three nights and not only did Jersey refuse to answer, he finally bat the telepathic reach away.

Telepathy with the Rakum wasn't complicated; every brother sees a filament connecting to his brother's psyche. Very young, a Rakum learns to grasp it in order to communicate. Jersey's method of repelling the seeking thread angered Emil who sent Kilmeade to find him and fetch him home.

Kilmeade found Jersey in the space of an hour and when Jersey refused to be returned, the two fought hand-to-hand in the moonlight. Expecting to be incapacitated by either a jolt or an unknown Elder-level move, the two wrestled for an hour, both lunging, ducking and striking, neither growing tired. Sweating and growing incrementally more determined, Jersey marveled at how the Candidate moved, slippery and quick, Kilmeade melted from Jersey's grasp every time he attempted a capture. After another thirty minutes, Jersey awoke to Kilmeade's scheme—the fight had been *foreplay*, the young Elder was busily *choosing* him. Elders need pups under them; was Jersey to be Kilmeade's first?

"But I have a master," Jersey said inside. Before he could ponder further, Kilmeade leapt into his space, clutched him tight, and drank his blood through a hasty knife-wound at the throat. Jersey was incapacitated and carried off to a different settlement. When he awoke, he began his life as Kilmeade's first pup...

"Being ish-mikhan isn't about fucking," his new master had told him soon after they reached his own estate in Sicily. "You know this, correct?"

Jersey watched his eyes, working up the best reply. Although Jersey had been with the Elder a fortnight, all his new master required him do so far was be nearby.

Kilmeade grinned and continued. "I will soon feel your hands on my flesh, your mouth, your lips everywhere a man feels pleasure. I know you want more than anything to see me happy."

"Yes, Master," Jersey said, stiffening below at the change of topic.

"But..." his master said with drama, his bright gray eyes holding Jersey fast. "Before we commence, you will learn about yourself. Lie here." Kilmeade gestured to the marble dining table to his right. The evening meal had been cleared and the serving staff dismissed. The only other person in the large candelabra-lit room was a soldier assigned to the door.

Without delay, Jersey hopped onto the cold stone and lay flat, emptying his mind as he'd been trained to do when time for a new lesson. Kilmeade chuckled softly as if amused by Jersey's thoughts, but there was nothing to be done about that. The young Elder opened Jersey's smock by loosening the tie strings at the neck and placed a cool palm to his sternum.

"Rest your concern, ish-mikhan. I find you alluring,"

Kilmeade said and Jersey turned his face. He had been wondering inside if he'd finally met a master that did not like his appearance. Kilmeade continued. "Like Emil, Gash, any number of the brethren who you've met, when I look upon you, I see the perfection of our race. More succinctly, a blue aura emanates from your outline and it soothes me."

"Yours is golden," Jersey said low, his throat suddenly raspy. "I have seen auras since my youth. Emil's is a rosy silver..."

Kilmeade's eyebrows raised a fraction and he smiled. "Ah, that is what I see. Now I am learning along with you."

He smiled then, his eyes twinkling with a new emotion Jersey did not know him well enough yet to name. Then, Jersey shivered, a growing urgency blossoming deep down. Kilmeade noticed and moved his hand to cover the fabric at Jersey's crotch, not pressing nor moving, only settled there, its presence increasing the insistent blood flow.

"Lust is a fog that suspends judgment and discernment," he cooed, purposefully using his silkiest voice. Jersey's body responded and he moaned. "I will teach you to harness it. You will enjoy incredible control over all those you entrance. Do you believe me?"

"Yes, Master," Jersey croaked and closed his eyes, commanding his body to return to plumb. Kilmeade didn't need fixing—he wanted to teach and learn. *"Wait, this is how I fix him— teach and learn, and he will be fixed."*

Kilmeade laughed aloud. "Yes!" he shouted and moved both hands to Jersey's cheeks. He leaned over to look into his face. "For now, let your lust be fulfilled with my lieutenant."

The soldier at the door headed over, seen to the side, and Jersey remained in Kilmeade's gaze.

"Pluto will fix you," his master said backing away. "And when I see you are deserving, we will dig into what else your master needs."

"Your will is my will," Jersey replied as Pluto appeared over

Kilmeade's shoulder.

The man was big, wide, sporting a bushy beard that surrounded ruddy cheeks. Kilmeade leaned against the wall, watching with a faraway look as Pluto jerked at Jersey's belt with rough hands. The soldier worked down Jersey's trousers and Jersey kept his eyes on Kilmeade. It was time to do whatever the master requested, and this heavy-handed grunt did what he could to relieve Jersey's distress.

Handed Off

Meeting Elder Roman

Year 1799

In 1799, Jersey hit the century mark and had discerned six months in advance that his master was preparing to hand him off. He knew from his youth that of all grunts, the ish-mikhan could expect to spend their entire lives moving from Elder to Elder. Some Rakum, especially the military types, remained with their first Elder for a lifetime, and others with a specific rare skill or eye-appeal were traded often. But the fix-it men expected to be transferred every few decades. Thus, when thirty years passed under Kilmeade's tutelage, Jersey looked with interest as to who his next master might be.

The night of *kazak*[7], Elder Roman arrived at Kilmeade's estate an hour past sundown, dressed in the highest fashion and traveling with his Rakum driver, who remained with the horses. This Elder was the same height as Kilmeade with similar hair and eyes, but Roman's personality was completely opposite his familiar master. From the first moment observing the Elder, Jersey noted Roman's tendency to remain faraway, his thoughts on something other than the present.

Every Elder had varying idiosyncrasies and discerning them was the ish-mikhan's vocation. Jersey hadn't met Roman; in his eighty-odd years plying his skill among the brethren, Elder Emil and then Kilmeade introduced him to fifty-five Elders and Elder-candidates. Tales and legends surrounding Elder Roman were few,

---

[7] Phrased this way, *kazak* (lit. "be strong," Hebrew; the common greeting among Rakum) refers to the night a grunt transfers to a new Pack.

so Jersey looked forward to seeing what he would learn upon their meeting. Having been summoned to the receiving lounge in time to see the Elder enter, he stood at ease at the back wall beside Darcy Vandiver, Kilmeade's second fix-it man and Jersey's closest companion.

After the two Elders greeted one another, they launched into discussions regarding issues important to their packs and the Rakum at large. Jersey wasn't mentioned and for ten minutes he and Darcy telepathically lobbed dirty limericks back and forth. When the topic finally spoke to Jersey's move, both Elders turned to face them and Kilmeade called them near.

"Brother, you shortchange yourself refusing this assignment," Kilmeade was saying to Roman as they reached position, stopping just within arm's reach. "You would have an excellent companion. Look at him—his top priority is your comfort."

"Please, Kilmeade—my decision stands." Roman remained resolute, but Kilmeade would not accept his flat refusal.

"You know I do not waste words. This one was well-instructed by Emil and in three decades, I have taken his training to the next level. No fix-it man in our history has learned what he has…"

The Elder paused with mystery and Roman, Jersey, and Darcy all turned to hear the rest.

"I have taught this one to work his trade flawlessly…"

Jersey flicked his eye to Darcy—they had discussed their master's novel approach at length. What Kilmeade meant, for the most part, was that Jersey had learned to follow his instincts *without question*. His discernment had reached such a level that he truly knew what an Elder wanted or would enjoy before the man himself. All ish-mikhan used techniques they judged an Elder might like, but Jersey's ideas would be more advanced, and he would proceed until physically stopped. Thus, like an Elder, he would trust his instinct 100% and assume he could never do wrong.[8]

---

[8] *("An Elder is never wrong." This is one of our tenets that we hold as fact.)*

Kilmeade continued. "He will know you better than you know yourself. Give him full rein and trust him. I will only ask once more. Are you certain you do not want Jersey to yourself?"

"Kazak," Roman responded as if impatient to depart. "I will escort him to Elder Kahn as agreed. Let us load up. The moon is high."

Kilmeade *tsked.* "You will do this one thing before handing him off," Kilmeade said and as Jersey looked on, his master put strong hands to the other Elder's shoulders, looking him in the eye. "You will allow him to show you his specialty. You are aware that if you say no…"

Kilmeade did not complete his threat and Jersey wondered what it might have been. Unlike most of the Elders he observed as they interacted with Kilmeade, this one was not cowed. On the contrary, Roman rolled his eyes and sighed. Jersey was pondering all these things when Roman's sharp gaze zoomed his way.

Kilmeade chuckled. "He knows Elders, Roman," Kilmeade said in a new laugh. "You're about to reveal our secret with this aloof affect."[9]

Roman shushed him and fixed Jersey with a stern eye. "Do not think on my business, pup. I do not easily disregard irreverent behavior, no matter how delightful you have been to Elder Kilmeade."

"Pish," Kilmeade whispered to them both and turned to face Jersey, his back to his fellow Elder. *"Roman is bluffing,"* he sent telepathically. *"Get him alone, away from the ears and eyes of your brethren and you will find him as appreciative as anyone."* Kilmeade backed and looked to Roman. "By the time you reach Kahn, you will say in Jersey's ear, 'Kilmeadz l'fhasz.'"[10]

Kilmeade had whispered the Rakum sentiment in an eerie

[9] *(By the time this book went to print, I discovered Roman was Kilmeade's fraternal twin, a detail they hid from the brethren their entire lives. Whatevs.)*

[10] Several sentiments rolled together here, basically meaning, "Kilmeade is correct in all things we have discussed."

undertone and Jersey forcibly suppressed a blush. The compliment was huge he held his face static, already reading that Roman did not want Jersey to express his joviality. Then, it was time to leave and call *kazak* to Darcy. On the way to the door, the conversation between the Elders amused Jersey and he smirked, aware Darcy heard from where he stood indoors.

Roman said, "One hundred Elders and you're the only one simultaneously holding two ish-mikhan. It is a waste."

Kilmeade chortled. "I disagree. They sharpen each other. Do you bunk your lieutenant with his captains so he may instruct and sharpen his inferiors?" Kilmeade's eyebrows arched and he chuckled when Roman looked away. "It is the same for my ish-mikhan." Kilmeade clapped Roman's back. "I know what I am doing at all times. You are aware of this."

"Yes, I am," Roman replied and boarded the carriage. He averted his gaze when Jersey piled in and settled across. The two Elders said no more, the horses surged forward at the driver's command, and Jersey exhaled. When two minutes elapsed, Roman's eye remained out the window to the dark night, his breathing slow and his pulse thumping in Jersey's ears.

Don't think on my business… Jersey considered the Elder's command. *But his business is my entire purpose.* The Elder only meant he didn't like Jersey's uninvited presumption. What had he been pondering when Roman grew agitated?

Oh, that he doesn't fear Kilmeade as the others—

"Are you so incorrigible?" Roman asked then, his gaze sharp in the dark interior. "You would repeat your error before five minutes has elapsed?"

"Master, if you will," Jersey answered his voice silky, "it is as if you requested I change my eyes from green to brown—I am not capable of thinking on anything *except* your business. For our journey, please send me out. It will give you peace." He used his eyes, submissive and adoring. Roman swallowed while holding Jersey's gaze, at first, revealing no evidence of being affected by his magnetism. Finally, his countenance softened and Roman leaned backward into the seat.

"Come close."

Jersey shifted his weight to swing over to the Elder's side of the carriage. Outside, the horses hit a spot of loose gravel and rocks hit the vehicle's underside as Jersey sat, now inches away. Roman had averted his gaze out the window, and without looking at Jersey, he pat his thigh.

"Lie here, face up."

Obediently, Jersey spun in place, positioning on his back. With his knees bent and heels to his buttocks, he rested his head atop the Elder's lap. Roman's face pivoted and he took one short glance of Jersey's scrunched body before meeting his eye.

"Sleep well, *polcz-v'.*"

Jersey closed his eyes and Roman's cool fingers cupped his outside cheek and then ran into his wavy hair. When the Elder's ribcage expanded with a breath of air, Jersey succumbed to the soothing energy flowing from Roman's palm and he was out.

A jostle to his shin brought him around and Jersey opened his eyes. The carriage had been parked and the horses sat in their traces, breathing soft puffs through velvety nostrils. Another poke and he turned his eyes to a brother with the duty to rouse him.

"Kazak, *kil-scez*,"[11] the youngster said and stepped back. "Your master is ready for you."

Jersey grinned at the compliment and clambered out to stretch. The position of the moon and purple horizon informed Jersey of the time and he followed the Rakum into a small dwelling. Without a word, the man led him to a hallway and then a closed door before turning, his hand on the brass knob.

"Master Roman is in the third room on the right."

---

[11] Literally, "delectable," as decadent and rare candies.

Jersey awaited more; the brother hadn't given his name, which would be the custom, and his respirations indicated he had additional comments. Jersey made a guess at his consternation and offered a new grin.

"You've never met a fix-it man?" he asked, his head to the side. The brother's unreadable expression remained static. He was young, maybe fifty, with large brown eyes, shaggy hair, and perfect bone structure. He smelled of sweat and leather and before Jersey could guess more, he inclined his head one nod.

"Name's Ivan. My captain has spoken of you. I didn't expect you to be so…" He paused, choosing his words. "So…" he said and pointed up and down Jersey's frame.

"Good or bad?" Jersey asked. *Who didn't love Jersey?*

Ivan smirked and didn't reply. Instead, he turned the knob which opened to a stairwell leading to an earthen cellar. Jersey couldn't allow his question to stand unanswered. He did not move when the brother gestured.

"Good or bad?" he asked again. If the man didn't fawn over him soon, he would get the full treatment.

Ivan rolled in his lips and clasped his hands behind his back, both standing before the blackness of the below. The Rakum's eyes laughed and Jersey watched him another few seconds. He was being baited—the youngster's captain must have put him up to it. Jersey sighed, so what? With a careful exhale, he grasped Ivan's gaze with invisible bonds. Then, without holding back, he thrust every ounce of his projection on to the man who, at only fifty, hadn't yet reached sexual maturity. The result must have been precisely what the man's captain had wanted; Ivan's eyes grew huge, his smirk disappeared, and both hands flew to his crotch, pressing and now falling to his knees. With a last whimper, the youngster looked away, slumped onto his buttocks on the rough wooden plank floor and waited for his erection to pass.

From below, boisterous laughter filtered to Jersey's ears. He pat Ivan's head and trotted into the dark. On the cellar floor, an oil lamp sat in the wall nook and he lifted it. Those laughing were further in and Jersey called a greeting as he searched the unfinished hiding place. The floor had been planked but the walls remained of stone and earth, with several rooms tunneled out for Rakum travelers. These waystations peppered the countryside of the entire continent, and this one was clean and smelled of dirt, not the rot and sewage of some others.

"Mighty shit! Master, don't torture us!" a deep voice called as Jersey reached his brethren. A circle of three Rakum captains filled the space and Jersey sensed Elder Roman near. The soldier who had spoken (and laughed earlier at the young one) stepped up and introduced the others. "That's Ollie, Pratt, and I'm Killian. Shit, Jersey, stand still a minute. Let me memorize you."

With raised eyebrows, Jersey stopped his forward movement, awaiting anything else. From the other room, Roman telepathically informed him that the men had been instructed "hands off," and for several evenings leading up to that edict, they had anticipated an all-out orgy when their VIP guest arrived.

Jersey met Killian's lurid gaze with an easy grin. He'd take care of all of them if commanded—he'd enjoy it—but their master had his reasons. Killian read all of this in Jersey's eyes and it didn't help him forget his broken plans.

"Shi-i-i-i-i-i-i-t!" he growled and tilted his chin toward the closed doors behind them. Jersey surmised he was speaking with Roman. His eye twitched once and he exhaled, his heart hammering. With one last expletive, Killian stepped aside, and Jersey passed, purposefully brushing his elbow to the soldier's bare forearm. A harmless electric shock passed between them and Jersey felt all three men watching him exit.

Inside the Elder's borrowed quarters, he found Roman sitting before a fire, undressed aside from a cloth across his lap, with a heated kettle of water on the hearth hook. He approached, and his master faced the flames.

"As long as we travel together, none of your brethren should

24

touch you," he said quietly and then turned to catch Jersey's eye.

Jersey nodded, seeing the disgust in the Elder's face. Most Elders did not share him with grunts. Any time he spent among his brothers occurred when his Elder was away on business. Plus, regarding Roman, he had heard rumors that the aloof and scholarly Elder had little use for grunts, Cows, or even women. He enjoyed his private time and his fellow Elders' company exclusively.

But Kilmeade said he would appreciate my attention, Jersey remembered and Roman saw it in his thoughts. He licked his lips once and turned back to the fire.

"Wash your master," he said flicking his gaze to the kettle. "Wash yourself, and then we will see what Elder Kilmeade is promising."

Jersey moved into position and squeezed out the sponge the Elder had placed in the heated water. "Your will is my will," he said, and meant every word.

The sun had set and Jersey reeled in his limbs in case he had assumed too much of the cot-like bed as he slept. He needn't have concerned himself; the Elder's side was cold and his master stood at the exit, eyes thoughtfully to the ceiling.

"Are you rested?" he asked.

Jersey read a new affinity in the Elder's gaze but squashed his thoughts. The mentally superior Rakum read them anyway and he huffed. As far as Jersey ascertained the evening had been a success. Once the coupling initiated, he did not ask for suggestions and Roman behaved as Kilmeade instructed, trusting Jersey would know more than he did about his duty. The final move of the evening, though, the Elder stepped out of what Jersey considered his character. When his master was prepared to finally release every ounce of lust carefully and methodically accumulated by Jersey's skill, he pressed his right palm to Jersey's flesh and shared the sensation to the last iota. Never in his life had he experienced such an explosion of pleasure and when the Elder ceased seizing and caught his breath, he had dropped his hand, pulled Jersey close to his body, and laughed loud and long.

"I only wish my brother Kilmeade had seen your face," he had said softly in Rakum Hungarian. He had chuckled a little more and then sat up to grasp Jersey's cheeks firmly with both hands. He jerked him close almost painfully, his mouth pressed hard against Jersey's. Then he whispered too low to hear without telepathy, *"Kilmeadz l'fhasz!"*

Jersey's gaze returned to his master, who was watching him, his expression was as stern as the night before, but with a new sparkle of respect for Kilmeade's ish-mikhan. Jersey cleared his mind as his thoughts irked the Elder's mood.

"The carriage is waiting—" he said, and Jersey's attention swiveled to the far wall, hearing a new voice. Roman sighed at his loss of focus and cleared his throat. "If you will allow me to finish—Elder Dawn and his Elder-candidate will complete your transaction to Kahn…"

Jersey looked back, hearing the end of the Elder's explanation in his mind: *I have been called away…* With a tiny nod, Jersey stood and began to dress. Roman watched him pull on his trousers and shirts, guarding his thoughts, but he did not look away until every garment had been adjusted.

A heavy footfall approached and a man barked in a voice of gravel at the soldiers outside the door. When he stepped in, Jersey's eyes widened. This Elder had to be the tallest he'd ever seen—taller than Darcy. He could have been 6'10" or 11", wide across the chest with skin so dark it barely reflected the light of the low lamps. He turned his face to Jersey after greeting Roman with a curt nod. A deep furrow snaked down his cheek, an injury inflicted before he was old enough to heal, and other than that distraction, he shone with the glory of any Elder.

"You're a tiny fuck, eh, ishy?" the master said, taking three long strides to stop in the center of the room. He didn't have to say it—the command "come close" was understood and Jersey had already begun the move. When in reach, Elder Dawn grasped Jersey's neck, his palm encircling his throat. The grip was gentle, though, despite its enormity and no doubt amazing strength. He pulled Jersey into his space and leaned down to bury his nose in Jersey's hair. Inhaling deeply, he sent telepathic messages to Jersey, testing their link. *"You're what? Six feet nothing? Can you fight? Do I need to worry over breaking you in half? Does Roman think I don't detect your scent all over his skin? You're pretty special, eh? My Elder-Candidate thinks he can resist you. What would you say if I asked you to tend my entire entourage at once?"* When his silent query-barrage ceased, he pulled back enough to look Jersey in the eye.

"Your will is my will," Jersey replied.

"Hah!" he said aloud and flicked his wrist in Roman's direction. "I accept custody, brother. *Kazak.*"

Elder Dawn never looked at the other master, but in his peripheral vision, Roman moved smoothly away. He sent Jersey a private *kazak* and was gone.

"Avel, enter and meet little Jersey," Elder Dawn said, his eyes in Jersey's and a mischievous grin in place. Around the Elder's gigantic arm, another man entered, this one no more than 6'2" with dark hair, bright brown eyes and swarthy appearance. His thick hair formed miniature ringlets and when he met Jersey's eye, he smiled.

"I have never seen a more perfectly formed face."

Dawn huffed and nodded, his fierce gaze as sharp as before, belying only his personality, not his state of emotion. "So, you will enjoy looking at him?"

"In the least," Avel answered and reached out his hand which Jersey grasped.

Behind the Elder-Candidate, the hallway had filled with Dawn's entourage plus the three-man duty-staff, one of them being Killian from the evening before. When their eyes met, the captain blew him a kiss. Without reaction, Jersey returned his focus to Avel who was busily examining his musculature with strong hands.

"Are all ish-mikhan this small?" he asked presumably Jack because Jersey didn't know. He'd met one, Darcy, who was 6'6".

Jack Dawn released Jersey's neck and ran his open palm down Jersey's sternum and then across his pecs. "Jersey's not small compared to you, idiot," the Elder rebutted and comically measured Avel's height to Jersey's. "Now, in front of everyone," he said with authority and glanced to every soldier present, "you boasted last evening you would have no problem resisting an ish-mikhan's wiles. Well, here he is. Face off. Show us how very powerful your will is."

Jersey tilted his chin to the junior Elder who didn't meet his eye. Instead, Avel's gaze roamed those of the men in attendance and landed in Jack's. "I remain as confident as before. How can a mere grunt manipulate me? I'm a goddamn Elder-Candidate, not a First-Rit moron."

Grumbles of agreement emanated from the others, but Jack Dawn commanded them be still. He positioned behind Jersey and clasped his shoulders, manually squaring Jersey to Avel. Leaning close, he whispered in Jersey's ear low enough to keep it private, "This is your test, too, ishy. Don't let me down."

Jersey licked his lips. Elder Dawn had to be pleased, satisfied, "fixed," and the current challenge was what he needed most. Jersey must succeed. He remembered Kilmeade's training and imagined his fingers just touching the sheath of Elder Dawn's mental thread. He caressed it, sending the sentiment, *Your will is my will, and it will be done.*

"Fuck me!" the Elder hissed under his breath and gave Jersey a little shake with the contact on his shoulders. In his normal volume he said, "Okay, hotshot, show me." To Avel, he said, "Do it now, you chickenshit. Look at him."

The Elder-Candidate had indeed been delaying. His eye went

to Jersey's cheek, still avoiding initiating the test. Jersey was ready, Master Dawn's pleasure his number one goal. He would not fail, he had no doubt, and to add to his master's enjoyment, he intended to push Avel further than he'd ever pushed anyone before.

"You're in trouble, Avel," Dawn whispered, apparently sensing or reading Jersey's thought-stream.

The underground hallway and room entrance fell silent. Avel swallowed and sucked his teeth before slowly turning his face to Jersey's. Jersey let him have it.

Every Rakum had special skill in *something,* and the past three decades with Kilmeade, Jersey had honed his into a weapon. Within the first second, the Elder-Candidate's eyes widened and went round. His breath caught, hitched once, and then exhaled in a whimper. Jersey held him fast. It was apparent from the first moment Avel hadn't been prepared—he had never met a fix-it man and had no defense. Jack Dawn must have known this, for even as Jersey continued to push him, sensing the man losing strength in his legs and about to go down, Dawn was snickering in Jersey's mind, *"heh heh heh heh heh, ishy, heh heh heh heh."*

"Pollllz," the Elder-Candidate garbled in their language and went to his knees, still locked in Jersey's gaze. Jersey sighed and the man jerked his face to the right, slamming his weight onto his palms to face the dirt floor. "FUCK! STOP!" he barked and the entire room caught the aroma of his seed as it left his body.

Jack Dawn laughed so loudly that Jersey and several soldiers covered their ears. He kissed the back of Jersey's head sending telepathically, *"What am I thinking?"*

As he'd been trained, Jersey responded the first thing that entered his mind. *"That you lost interest in copulation seven centuries ago but are interested in seeing me educate the brethren tonight."*

Jack nodded, his face still in contact with Jersey's wavy hair. *"If there is time, I would spar with you, see what Emil and*

Kilmeade taught you in the circle of battle, but tonight…"

Of its own accord, Jersey's mind pictured himself and the gigantic Elder in hand-to-hand combat. At the same time, intuition told him that Jack Dawn would enjoy bringing him to the edge of death and reviving him—more than once, if possible; that he practiced this with his top soldiers—at least the ones sturdy enough to bounce back without permanent injury.

Behind him still, the Elder *tsked* in his ear. *"Focus, ishy and look at these men. None have known or even met a fix-it man. It is my will that you spend this evening with them—make certain each goes to sleep with a smile."* He inhaled in Jersey's hair one more time and said aloud, "You have made me proud."

Yet on the ground and now lying on his side, Avel worked up a few words. When his throat cleared, he sought Jersey's eye and sent telepathically, *"I am also proud of you and what you have accomplished. Next time, I will be ready. Kazak."*

Jersey sent him a respectful nod; after all, eventually, he would be a full Elder and Jersey longed to see him just as satisfied as his master.

"Killian," Jack barked, still standing behind Jersey, "show the ishy to your quarters and return him to Avel before sunup." Then his voice lowered, the direction telling Jersey he now faced Avel who was rising to his feet. "At sunup, he will bunk with you. Try not to embarrass me in the future." Without a word, the junior Elder nodded and Jack belted Killian's name again.

With a smile that could grow no wider, the man wove his way from behind his brothers and gently grasped Jersey's bicep. As the highest-ranking soldier in the group, Killian would call the shots, even over Jack Dawn's entourage. "This way, Jersey," he said, his deep voice nearly laughing.

Jersey allowed himself to be led in the captain's guiding grip and when they had crossed the length of the earthen tunnel system, they reached a large barracks. Ten men collected in the anteroom where several cots and chairs scattered, and Killian stopped before the door of an inner room which contained a small feather-mattressed bed. He released Jersey and faced the men. Jersey stood abreast, having read the captain's next command for the men. Killian sensed his mental intrusion, but allowed it, probably hoping to gain favor for their future interaction. *"I have specific inquiries that only you can answer,"* he sent while facing the soldiers. *"Tell them what to do next."* Then the captain cleared his throat and the whispering brethren grew quiet.

"Jersey will tell you how to proceed." Killian stepped back. With a small nod, Jersey exhaled, his plans formed.

"Everyone except Killian remove your shirt," he said and waited as they did as instructed.

Tending several at once was not uncommon and Jersey had already devised the best way to satisfy each man individually and within the time allotted. He stepped to the first brother and after putting a flattened palm to his chest, he sought the identification of the one among them he liked the most. An image arose of the soldier to his right.

"Pavel, you're with Bascom," he said and pointed to the other wall. The two men stepped off and he went down the line. All the remaining brethren were similarly paired until he reached Ivan, the same one who had experienced his power the night before.

"I will see you alone," Jersey told him and then addressed the others. "Killian and I will visit privately, and when he exits, send in Ivan. When he exits, you decide who comes in next and do it in pairs, as I assigned you."

Every man consented and Jersey ignored the frowns of some who did not like having to wait. Behind him, Killian opened the door to the inner room and stood by. Jersey followed him in and he closed the heavy oak with a definitive noise. Barely had Jersey pivoted to face him and the captain advanced.

"I learned as a youth that the *ish-mikhan's* telepathy works differently than the rest of us," he said, opening a dialogue while advancing in such a way that Jersey was inclined to step the equal number of steps backward. It wasn't aggression, but foreplay, which Jersey saw clearly in Killian's mind. "I see your thread," the man said. "It looks perfectly normal. Tell me what's different."

Jersey's backside met the hastily plastered wall and he allowed his head to rest against it. He met Killian's eye.

"It's a show, not a tell," he said, his voice soft, beginning the dance. Killian stopped mere inches away and used both strong hands to tug and then remove Jersey's smock and inner shirt.

"Show," the captain whispered and leaned in too close to see.

Jersey considered his mental thread, gleaming with information ready for the picking to any Rakum brave enough to poke around. In his mind's eye, Jersey lifted an imaginary feather to the silvery fiber and delivered a single stroke. Like the Elder, Killian's reaction was immediate. With a sharp curse of surprise, he leaned out to see Jersey's face. Their eyes locked another long moment and Killian grinned.

"Do that again, slower," he whispered, and Jersey complied. "Impressive."

The captain released a careful exhale rearranging his thoughts. He trained his gaze to Jersey's now-bare chest and opened his hand against it. When he ran his palm down the center in a lethargic dragging fashion, he tucked his fingers just below Jersey's waistband and sought his eye once more.

"My second question," he rasped, his voice rumbling with testosterone, "are you beautiful because you are *ish-mikhan* or are you *ish-mikhan* because of your face?" He looked at his hand and added before Jersey could reply, "Is this magnetism the same for all of you?"

Jersey turned his face to the side knowing Killian would move in to kiss his throat.

"We look normal, like the rest of you, but because of our nature, we appear almost glorious. We think…" Jersey paused as the captain's caresses grew in intensity. The soldier planned to bring the pleasure-giver pleasure before receiving his due. It was a rare approach, but Jersey had no complaints. He swallowed and completed his thought with, "I think we look to you like the Elders look to the *ish-mikhan*."

Killian grew quiet, hard at work undressing them both. Then he said, "If you see Jack Dawn the way I see you..." he chuckled before continuing, "...that's just fucked *wayyyyyyy* up."

Jersey huffed. "You're blind if you can't see how glorious he is. How perfect, how..." The captain's hand moved in just the right way that Jersey stopped volunteering conversation.

"This..." Killian ran his hand down Jersey's cheek but was not looking into his face, rather his eyes were riveted to the work his other hand attended. "This is glorious, *you*... are splendid..."

Jersey's eyes fell closed to the sensations the captain aroused, but Killian was moments from voicing his next thought. Jersey beat him to it, hoping to bring the talking to a close.

"Your will tonight is for me to remember you after I'm long gone, for me to consider you one of my favorite fucks..." Jersey paused, but there was more. He continued, "You want to see the pleasure on my face and know you brought it..."

Jersey shivered with desire and Killian chuckled, waiting for him to read the rest of his thought. Jersey's tongue froze and he sent the last telepathically.

"You will learn from me some new things which you will practice on those you fuck in the future..." Jersey gasped, finished reading and done thinking altogether.

Killian said in his mind, *"Yes, yes, yes, and yes,"* and maneuvered Jersey toward the lumpy mattress. With a sudden strong-arm move, he forced him to lie down. Without another word, the soldier did his best to prove to the *ish-mikhan* that he could fix the fix-it man. And because of his skill and passion, he trusted Jersey would give him the highest marks.

Only ten minutes of the night remained, the sun's rays already peeking past the horizon. All Rakum were underground, but each man felt at a cellular level the sun bursting into the world.

Once every soldier had been attended, Killian guided Jersey to the Elders' quarters, this time walking behind with a palm to Jersey's lower back. He reached the outer door and didn't meet Jersey's eye when he turned for final words.

"Inside, my men left a kettle of water on the fire. If the masters require you to wash…" He left his remark open and with a parting *"kazak,"* he turned and disappeared down the dark hallway. Jersey reached for the knob, but the door swung open on its own.

"Come close, pup," Avel said from somewhere in the dark room. "I am not offended by your aroma. Come now."

Jersey crossed the room by feel, waiting for a light. As his toe bumped a low rug, a candle flamed to life and he saw clearly the Elder-Candidate lounging on a long velvet chaise.

"Sit here," he said putting his feet to the floor and then gesturing to the space his legs had been.

Jersey complied, studying his face and seeking his thread.

"I feel you working to divine my thoughts." Avel watched him settle in and turn partway so they could converse. "Only an Elder would dare peek into my head, so I was taken off guard when you grasped my thread without permission. Elder Dawn allowed it, which taught me another new thing."

He chuckled with a small head shake and Jersey narrowed his eyes. Hours ago, he recognized the Candidate's general physical description, but now, in such intimate quarters, a lightness hit his middle when the man's hair, an onyx mass of soft black ringlets, moved as independent creatures with every gesture of the Candidate's head. In another millisecond, Jersey realized what caused his fugue—the man would be an Elder, and that was all the magic an ish-mikhan would ever need to see beyond the physical world.

"Tell me," Avel said then, his tone urgent and his eyes seeking the answer in Jersey's mind. "What do you see?"

Jersey ran one hand in a semi-circle before his eyes and framing the Candidate's face. "I see the Elder in you," Jersey replied in a whisper. Avel's face read, *and that means?* Jersey sought the correct words for what truly had no verbal expression.

"Try, ishy, try," Avel said playing but serious.

"The first time I saw an Elder," Jersey began in a halting tone, trusting his instincts and wondering what he was about to say, "I saw this, what I see around you. None of the grunts have it, none."

Jersey licked his lips and enjoyed the eagerness for knowledge reaching Avel's eyes. The youth might not graduate to Elder for decades, but he was Elder enough for Jersey.

Avel grinned, a deep dimple in his right cheek. In a smooth and urgent movement, he cupped Jersey's throat and closed his eyes. Jersey felt his ethereal presence, whispering across his psyche, leaving him lightheaded and hard as a rock.

"Utterly amazing," Avel said in his mind. *"This is how you see me? Us? Your Elders?"* he continued and Jersey nodded. A tiny noise squeaked in Jersey's throat and Avel dropped the contact. "I need much more than a single day with you. I will request a week, a month, a year." The Candidate giggled then, silly and tilting his chin. "I am learning so many new things. Ishy things." He fixed Jersey with a new gaze. "What is my will tonight?"

Like a painting being created before his eyes, Jersey saw what the young master had in mind for their time together. Avel laughed with a single clap of his hands.

"Yes! You will teach me how to resist the *ish-mikhan*." Avel watched his eyes and in an instant, Jersey had formulated a lesson plan. Avel thumped his nose. "So, it can be learned."

"Yes, Master," Jersey said in earnest.

"Excellent." Avel leaned into the crook of the chaise end-arm and lifted a single leg to prop one foot on the cushioned seat, his knees splayed. "Can it be learned in one sitting?"

"Yes, but lying down," Jersey replied, hoping the Candidate asked no questions as to why they retire to the bed. It had little to do with the instruction, but more with how easy it would be to doze off once the young master was satisfied.

Avel scrunched his nose, reading his weariness. "Lean into me," he said, his arms open and welcoming.

With a huff of happy surprise, Jersey complied, swiveling his body until he sat between Avel's open thighs to lean his back to the Candidates strong chest.

"Begin." The master wrapped both arms about Jersey and rest his chin on his inner shoulder. "Teach me to resist."

Jersey took a deep breath and began, enjoying the way Avel raised his upper body to accommodate his movement. Resisting an *ish-mikhan* was possible and he'd gladly instruct the master on how it was done. *"But he'll never want to use it with Jersey,"* he thought and Avel laughed, this time, louder and with a jovial, friendly quality.

"No, again, you are correct," Avel returned in his head. With a butterfly's weight, he kissed Jersey's ear tip. *"Already my body is wondering what magic you are hiding. Get on with the teaching and I will get on with my learning. Before the end of the evening, both of us will be smiling."* And Jersey made sure his master was fixed, in whatever way he required.

Darcy

Vandiver

That font is sized at 100. If you knew Darcy the way I do, you'd fill an entire library simply writing his name. No shit. ~ Jersey

Darcy Vandiver came into the world in 1710. A mortal once asked me why some of us have a single name and some have more. The brethren are named by the Rakum physicians. A brother pops out and the doc assigns him a moniker. They had that authority. Get over it.

~ Jersey

Darcy Vandiver
Identified Late

Year 1719

It was 1719 when Darcy discovered he was ish-mikhan. Deep in the forests of Moldavia, the group lair had six residents, four of those being proselytes. At age nine, Darcy was the oldest. Most Rakum are assigned a life-track, identified by their proctors by age eight. As fate would have it, Darcy's eighth year came and went, and because of his size—he had grown to five feet before age seven—his superior pegged him as a soldier and looked no more into it.

The proctor, Larp Nightly, hailed from Greece and kept to himself beyond his official lair duties. Any lesser tasks fell to his second, Cho-Now, a twenty-five-year-old First-Rit new graduate whose life-track revealed he'd proctor youths himself one day. Two centuries old, Larp was big with a barrel chest and thick, muscular thighs. Cho-Now stood nearly as tall, but being young, remained lithe and well-defined without any bulk. Both were experts at hand-to-hand combat and pummeling the unusually tall Darcy Vandiver had become the highlight of most evenings. As a result, neither adult spent time with Darcy outside of mandatory lessons and recreational sparring. Because of this, Darcy spent the lion's share of his free time studying.

Enter Elder Pebb. Tall and strong, with a trim and hard

midsection which he accentuated with tailored waistcoats and snug silk trousers. Many males of that era wore their hair to their shoulders, but Pebb trimmed his black locks above his ears to better frame his high cheekbones and bring out his severe azure eyes.

Master Pebb kept a vast residence in Hungary and one evening, as the story goes, the Ten Fathers sensed a need to investigate Larp's lair. With his geographic position being closest, Elder Pebb assumed the assignment, hoping to find a new brother of interest or talent that he might bring home. Pebb had reached four centuries and kept a thriving household of Rakum with varying talents using each to the extent of their abilities.

Darcy had been eating the evening meal with the other youths when Master Larp's booming voice commanded all four to join him in the meeting hall. As the senior student, Darcy took the lead while the others followed by order of age. When he rounded the pillar to the room, his eyes landed on their visitor, the first Elder Darcy had ever seen. For the first three seconds, he didn't breathe, his eyes locked to the Elder's profile as he spoke to Larp and Cho-Now. Pebb's outline shimmered in Darcy's vision, waves of indeterminate substance rippled outward. *How does he emanate that light?* Darcy had not expected to see something so miraculous and so far, he hadn't known such a thing existed. *This is a brother, right? What is that light?*

Darcy hadn't breathed and still in profile, the Elder nodded to Cho-Now. *Do not turn, oh, please do not turn,* Darcy said inside, certain that he would lose consciousness if he looked in the eyes of anyone carrying such a full-body halo.

"...four pre-rits..." their proctor was saying, his hand gesturing to Darcy's position.

Here it comes, he's going to see... He's going to see me...

Master Pebb's face turned to the youths and as the senior student, he met Darcy's eye first.

Darcy's world went black.

"How could we know?"

Master Larp's voice. Darcy creaked open his eyes and the Elder's beautiful face filled his vision.

"Those eyes…" Larp continued. "I see it now. I'm blind as shit."

Darcy did not avert his attention from the Elder.

"Me, too. I'd have fucked him every night," Cho-now said and Larp agreed with a laugh.

It was time to rise and attend whatever his masters required. Darcy struggled to find his feet, but the Elder stilled him.

"Kazak, Darcy Vandiver," Pebb said in an incredible silky voice, his silvery-blue eyes mesmerizing Darcy to the core.

Darcy did not move and took stock of his person. He lay partly across the Elder's lap, them both on a soft feather mattress. Darcy had never seen this room, but he did not investigate more than enough to know it was unfamiliar. Instead, he held the Elder's gaze, wishing with all his being to disappear in the space where he and the master could be one creature.

Pebb grinned then, wide and showing white teeth. *"We are One already, little brother,"* Darcy heard in his mind, the master's telepathic voice like water on a scorched tongue. *"And now that I have found you, we will only grow closer."* With one hand, he stroked Darcy's cheek and then ran his fingers into his long hair.

"Still… ish-mikhan? All this time? Un-fucking-believable."

That was Cho-Now, but Darcy did not turn. Whatever had the adults so entranced mattered not. Darcy only wanted to know more about the Elder. Even before he could complete his pondering thought, the master's mental thread came into view, not silver like the others in the house, but metallic gold, and it emanated light that he had never seen in any of the Rakum he'd met in his short life. With the Elder smiling on him and now sending a tiny nod which carried the sentiment, *"go ahead, see what happens",* Darcy drew in his bottom lip and imagined touching that thread.

"Ah!" Darcy gasped aloud and in his peripheral vision, Larp and Cho-Now backed away. Elder Pebb leaned down and pressed his lips to Darcy's forehead.

"You are coming with me. Tonight. Gather your belongings."

Darcy saw in the master's mind a long carriage ride and then an enormous castle. Inside, a hundred brethren awaited their master's return and all of them would cheer when introduced to Darcy Vandiver. For the first time since meeting the Elder, Darcy grinned. In his master's mind, the brothers were going to receive Darcy as if he was special, unique, and valuable.

"I am not just a soldier; I am something much more," he said in his heart and mind, not planning to, but continued with, *"You are so beautiful, Master..."*

Elder Pebb nodded with a new grin and stood, setting Darcy to his feet. "Go now, do as I commanded."

Darcy trotted off, barely noticing his three brethren watching the events with wonder. In another ten minutes, he had climbed into Pebb's carriage with a single carry-sack at his feet.

"This is Adonis, he will be your proctor," the master said pointing a knuckle to a squat and handsome brother sitting on the opposite side of the carriage. "He has trained three *ish-mikhan* up to First Ritual. You will reside with him for three years, but when year thirteen is upon you, Darcy Vandiver is mine."

Darcy grinned again, completely enamored with the master's brilliant eyes. The sensations bubbling from his deepest parts were new, the most persistent one being a visceral desire to see Elder Pebb proud of him. Before tonight, Darcy served as his *duty.* But now? For the first time, he sensed a selflessness, a mortal attribute that had always been severely frowned upon by his race. Darcy's smile flickered. *Does that mean I am weak?*

Pebb chuckled then and grabbed him close by both shoulders. After staring into his eyes, he reeled him in, maneuvering Darcy's tall body into his lap as before, half across Pebb's thighs and the other filling the coarse bench seat.

"Shhhh," Pebb said, his lips pressed into Darcy's reddish-brown hair. "Lesson Number One, polcz-v', this is who you are—let it flow. When the urge to serve combines with one of your Elders, follow your inner muse." Darcy's current position meant he faced Adonis, who attended the interaction in silence. He wanted to see Master Pebb; should he pivot? Rough fingers grabbed the crown of his head then and the Elder physically swiveled his upper body. "Listen to your instincts," Pebb hissed with a flare of anger.

"Yes, Master," Darcy returned. At the Lair, he was taught the opposite—resist a first thought and work through each issue with care. Incorrect answers brought painful punishment, and although even a nine-year-old Rakum appreciated the life-affirming sensations of torture, Darcy never liked disappointing his superiors.

With his face to the Elder's, Adonis said across the space, his voice urgent, "You are not like the other Pre-Rits, Darcy. Right now! Do not think! Look deep inside, ask yourself, 'what would make my master proud?'"

Darcy licked his lips and repeated the question in his mind. Although difficult, he pushed back the voice of his former proctor commanding he shut up and stand still. Another voice whispered, one that had been hiding in Darcy's heart and he sensed it peeking out, looking both ways, and crawling up his throat. The master held him close, face-to-face, his eyes as deep as the ocean and expecting the young proselyte to do something amazing.

The voice inside gave Darcy an idea and he lifted his outside hand to the Elder's face. Running the hand across Pebb's whiskered chin he cupped the muscular neck and tugged. The master offered no resistance but sunk lower until their mouths touched. Darcy had never kissed even for fun, there had been no stimulus to do so, and even as he rest his lips soft to his master's, he did not know how to proceed.

It doesn't matter what you know or don't know, perfect one. Everything will be given to you and you will one day rule your world with finesse and skill...

The voice of his muse. It was wise and it told him to use his tongue. Darcy and the master grinned at the same time. Darcy Vandiver had found his purpose and he was happy.

Darcy's First Elder

Brothel Lessons

Year 1745

On the evening of Darcy's thirteenth year, Proctor Adonis delivered him to Castle Pebb with fanfare and a feast suited for royalty. From age nine to thirteen, he often visited the master's bedchamber, but was returned before sunup to bunk with his proctor. Moving in and spending every waking moment in the Elder's glorious company kept Darcy eager to attack each new task. At thirty, the master began sending him to brothels to practice his technique. Tonight, Master Pebb's grin could grow no wider so Darcy knew he had done well. An hour earlier when his Elder deposited him into the dark and musty brothel, he hadn't realized how easy his assignment would turn out to be.

"The boy! I want the boy!"

The sentiment echoed in Darcy's mind, spoken by every man and woman seeking physical attention. The brothel owner served the Rakum and therefore, allowed Darcy to make the choice. Oh, the fun of turning the tables on the stupid blood-bags each expecting only carnal fulfillment.

"Line them up," Darcy whispered to the keeper as eleven mortal patrons argued over who would buy time with the beautiful boy with the long, cinnamon hair. He appeared barely fourteen to human eyes but was tall—over six feet and still growing. Adonis and Master Pebb had been diligently developing his musculature, so he was strapping, balanced head-to-toe with muscle, his adolescent shoulders round and thick. When the patrons heard

44

Herr Ingle's instructions, each one turned angry words and threats his direction.

"Line up or exit," the keeper told them in an even tone, not cowed. "This boy is special; you can all see it. Line up; he will choose his companions."

Still cursing, one-by-one, the patrons shuffled to the wall in a loose firing line, eyes seeking Darcy's. He stood in the center watching them assemble. None of them were attractive, none smelled clean, and Darcy found none of them appealing.

So... how to choose, he mused. Tonight's lesson was about manipulating and controlling mortals; there would be no need to undress or even touch them, except to draw the winner's blood.

What criteria would most please Master Pebb? Strength and size.

Darcy eyed the line-up left to right. Then his mouth formed a small grin. "That one," he said low and met the bloated tick's eye.

A rumble of frustration filled the room as the keeper ushered the unchosen to the next room where the hired prostitutes waited. The one Darcy had chosen remained, grinning and wringing his cap in his dirty and callused hands. Herr Ingle stepped close enough to the blob to receive his coins and then turned for the rooms.

With a questioning pause, the mortal watched Darcy, unsure if he should lead or follow. Darcy held a fathomless gaze which the man deciphered to mean he should go first. Once he waddled behind the brothel keeper, Darcy brought up the rear. He always kept them in front—never trust a mortal to stand behind you—one of Master Pebb's more recent lessons.

On a similar learning experience, the master brought Darcy and Adonis to a rowdy drinking establishment. Whomever Adonis chose, Darcy was to overcome. His proctor called it, "smash, fuck, drink, and strangle." In their language, *Jus, polt, va'* and *gyu*, the anacronym—*Jolvag*—formed the Rakum word for "laugh." This tickled their master and the night in question, he sent his servants in for a "laugh" that he would experience vicariously from the castle. *"Never let a mortal stand behind you,"* came into play when the man Adonis picked out stabbed Darcy in the back, driving his hunting blade four inches deep. Adonis ended the mortal in a heartbeat but was forced to carry Darcy to the carriage bleeding and mostly unconscious. When they returned to the master, Pebb healed his ish-mikhan's wounds, but didn't let him forget how his carelessness ruined a perfectly well-laid evening. Tonight, again his master expected diversion, and Darcy would make certain everything transpired as planned.

The brothel keeper pushed open a door at the end of the south hallway and stepped well back. Was he shying from Darcy? Probably. Ingle was a Cow, but his master was a Rakum named Oman whom Darcy had seen strike Ingle with an open hand on several occasions.

I'm not going to hit you, Darcy said internally, of course, not to the man, but he did stop in his face. Ingle's eyebrows went up and he leaned back.

"Anything else, Master?" he whispered so the patron wouldn't hear. "Is this okay?"

Darcy lowered his chin and batted his lashes, aware he was perceived as a harmless child to his chosen lout, but this Cow knew better. Darcy brought up his hand to touch Ingle's cheek, slowly so as not to frighten him further.

"I'm a friend, Herr Ingle," Darcy said in a quiet tone and held the man's gaze. Ingle was Darcy's height and although fifty-two, he remained strong and healthy in a village where many men died before that mark. "I like your face, but not your expression. When our eyes meet, I want to see joy, an eagerness to see me happy." Darcy stepped into his space and tenderly cupped his cheeks with both hands. "Do you want to see me happy?"

"Yes, Master," Ingle replied breathless.

Darcy leaned close and allowed his lips to barely touch Ingle's cheek, then he remained there, his breathing feathering on the man's ruddy jaw. "If I were to kiss you, would your expression change? Would I see in your eyes affection and allegiance?"

Darcy had whispered against the man's ear and Ingle held his breath, his heart beating faster than ever. With a small movement, an inch to his right and Darcy touched his lips to Ingle's, not pressing the kiss in, but waiting for the man to exhale. In less than three seconds, Ingle did, and Darcy pressed in, sealing their connection so the mortal's breath released entirely into Darcy. When he pulled back, he licked his lips and remained close, looking the man in the face and feeling his full-blown arousal in the contact their embrace caused from the waist down.

"There it is," Darcy whispered in the same impossible tone, holding Ingle's brown eyes in his. The man's entire body thrummed with unexpended energy and he worked up a response, licking his lips several times before he did so.

"Master, what can I do for you? You only have to ask."

Ingle had spoken soft so the patron wouldn't hear, but behind them and waiting in the room, the fat man commanded that he hurry. Darcy grinned at Ingle and the man exhaled again, his shoulders dropping and his eyes wet with tears.

"I want to see this face every time I visit," Darcy said and backed away, only dropping contact when at arm's length. Ingle offered an effusive nod, his eyes declaring a dedication that no amount of Oman's abuse could lessen. Darcy turned and entered, closing the door in the keeper's face.

"Enough of that shit! Get over here!" the fat customer barked watching Darcy secure the lock and face him in the dim room. "You will earn your silver tonight, young man, and you will learn to obey," he added, working his belt loose.

Darcy held up one hand, palm out. "You might want to keep those on," he said planning the first move and working out the various scenarios that could follow. A puzzled frown hit the man's round face before he yanked his leather belt free. He flicked it through the air to create a snap and sent Darcy a grin.

"I like that game, too," he said and whipped the thong through the air a second time, not advancing, but he widened his stance.

With a strategy in place, Darcy surged forward and slammed into the patron's flabby embrace. In three well-executed movements, the man was dropped to the floor, face down with one arm securely rammed behind his own back. Darcy shoved a rag deep into his mouth and allowed him to gag and struggle a full minute. Then the man grew tired, stopped resisting and relaxed under Darcy's weight.

It was time to take his blood. Darcy considered his preferred drawing spot, but on a man so large, the neck had zero appeal. There was the crook of the arm... Darcy wrinkled his nose. He didn't want his mouth on the guy at all.

"You would waste all that perfectly good blood, pup?" Elder Pebb asked in his mind, enjoying the show from miles away.

"I think I will, Master," Darcy returned, his lip in a snarl at his victim's aroma. *"He's only one mortal; there are millions more."*

In his mind, his master chuckled and slithered away. Was Pebb impressed or disappointed? Darcy couldn't tell. With one more run at imagining what it might be like to put his lips on the man to draw blood, Darcy made a decision and in one swift move, broke his neck. His Elder transmitted no reaction, so Darcy stood to drag the dead man to the far wall. The brothel keeper would help him dispose of the corpse.

Wait... Ingle is a Cow! Darcy grinned at the thought of the man's blood rushing down his throat.

"So now you would tap Oman's Cow?" Master Pebb sent with humor.

Darcy pictured the tall brown Rakum with the fierce expression. He was there, somewhere in the brothel. He'd had no interactions with the brother, but knew he came from Emil's pack and that was a great honor. He opened the door to the hall and called Ingle's name. In another minute, the man entered, and

Darcy closed them in. The expression he'd left Oman's Cow with a half-hour before remained. Ingle *loved* him. *A lot.*

"I need help dumping that guy's body and I need your blood." Darcy looked into his face at the second phrase and Ingle was nodding and already unbuttoning his shirt. Darcy flashed his eyes in appreciation and drew close, his knife making a swift wound. Ingle remained still, arms at his sides, but harder than ever below. Darcy couldn't see the man's thread, he tried. But if he could, he would have toyed with perhaps taking their interaction further.

In his mind, Master Pebb *tsked* at his thought-stream. *"Drink your brother's Cow, fuck your brother's Cow. Ingle's blood-scent has reached Oman's nostrils. You have less than a minute..."*

Still, the master did not sound perturbed and Darcy closed his mouth, healing the wound with the pad of his thumb.

"I will enjoy seeing how you deal with Oman," his master sent at the last and was gone.

To Ingle, he whispered, "Drag him out the back. Your master's headed in and he's not happy about our love affair."

Herr Ingle expressed a few different emotions at his words, but got to work, hefting and yanking the dead man out the back entrance of the room, only looking away from Darcy when time to close the hall door.

Here we go, Darcy said to himself and Master Pebb heard it, too. He ran down scenarios, similarly as he did with the client, but with Oman, the outcomes favored his opponent. The Rakum might attack him without a word—Darcy had broken a well-established tenet about the sanctity of holding Cows. Or his brother might be charmed—their interaction might end with laughter and discussion. And the last possibility, and probably the least likely, he'd use his *ish-mikhan* strengths. Darcy was a new presence among the local packs and only one other Elder besides Pebb knew he was there. In addition, unless someone had a reason to tell him, Oman wouldn't necessarily know Darcy's status. He sent a query to his master but received back the same sentiment as before: "this will be fun to watch."

The door across the room swung wide and Oman stood in the opening, his eyes narrowing as he sought Darcy's gaze.

"Let me get this straight," he said when they locked eyes. He entered and slammed the door. Two more steps forward, he stopped and crossed thick arms at his chest. "You're all of what? Thirty years old? And you decided I'm lacking as a master to my Cows? Your arrogance is well advanced."

Darcy's mouth formed a half-grin and he thrust his hands in his pockets. Oman had issued questions—he was a talk-first type. Darcy held the man's eye and shrugged his shoulders to his ears.

"I like him," he said with a new grin, "and I thought it might make you come here so I could meet you."

Oman blinked and, in another moment, he uncrossed his arms. "Why did you want to meet me? Aren't you Pebb's little proselyte? The one he's been teaching brothel techniques?"

"I am Master Pebb's ish-mikhan," Darcy said, watching for anything to register in Oman's gaze. This brother was at least a century-and-a-half old and would have learned of the rare brethren skilled in such things.

"No shit?" he said softer and stepped closer. "I never met a fix-it man," he added and again came closer.

Darcy held his eye and when Oman looked away, he scanned Darcy's body. He completed his approach and stood before him, his eyes returning to Darcy's.

"So that's why I'm not mad, eh?" he said very low, his mind apparently tracking over the past minute's conversation. "I looked at your face and wasn't even the least bit upset." He grinned now, his white teeth contrasting against skin as dark as cocoa. "That face… shit." The brother rolled in his bottom lip and held it with his upper teeth. His eyes flit now between Darcy's lips, eyes, and chest. "I'd enjoy that face in my lap."

Darcy widened his eyes. "Did I offend you, Master?"

"Fuck, yeah. You offended me. I'm immensely offended," he

said smiling and he lifted his hand to Darcy's smooth cheek.

"*Uh-oh,*" Darcy whispered with false trepidation. "*I messed up.*"

"*So, fix it, fix-it man,*" Oman said just as low and licked his lips. "I'm ready. Fix it." And Darcy leaned in.

When Oman left the room, Master Pebb wasn't the only one *very* impressed with Darcy Vandiver.

Famous

Darcy Transferred to Kilmeade

Year 1781

The moon sat high and full as Darcy's brothers packed the cart, the escorts' luggage consuming most of the space. Darcy only required a small bag containing his toiletries and a change of clothing.

He rubbed his chin in thought. He had turned seventy and Master Pebb said it was time to move on. He would serve Elder Emil in Italy and Darcy looked forward to meeting the famous master. Because he was ish-mikhan, Pebb assigned Darcy a complement of soldiers to ensure he would not be slowed down. It was assumed no matter what edict an Elder pasted upon his ward, Pebb's precious fix-it man must make it to his destination safely and on time. Lonely brothers were not the only concern, bands of human raiders often struck carriages that traveled through the wee hours of the night. A Rakum could best any mortal who attacked him. A Rakum Darcy's age and size could defend himself against as many as five healthy humans. Still, the trip would take several weeks, and protection remained a mandatory component of such a transfer. A dozen meters away checking the traces, Alnot turned in Darcy's direction.

"What're you thinking about, Darss?" he asked and ambled close. "You're about to pop a vein in your forehead." He laughed and pressed the pad of his thumb to the center of Darcy's brow.

Darcy ignored him; this was a brother he wouldn't miss. Tarn and Gilmore appeared from the other side of the wagon and he waved them over. These two had grown close, they were compatible and Master Pebb enjoyed watching them interact in whichever way his whims might take him. Tarn punched his shoulder when he got close and tossed him a grin.

"Kazak, Darss. We'll see you again," he said and looked at Gilmore. It was his turn and he chose to bump foreheads. He didn't say anything, but his eyes repeated their brother's sentiment. The senior brother at the reins barked for him to load up. Darcy stepped forward and a heavy hand landed on his shoulder from behind. He turned to face his master.

"You make me proud," Elder Pebb said squeezing both of Darcy's shoulders once, then allowing the contact to remain. "You'll make your new master even more so; I have no doubt."

"Kazak, Master," Darcy said low, he had no other words. He'd been happy here, he enjoyed his work, his brethren, his master, but he had expected to be moved around. Pebb held him close much longer than he ever expected. At that moment, the Elder sighed and ran both hands up Darcy's shoulder to encompass his neck.

"I have memorized you, polcz-v'. Over sixty-two years, twenty-thousand times have you serviced your master. I remember every moment."

Darcy held his face but his eyes grew round. All Rakum possessed perfect recall and would never forget anything of importance. If someone asked him how many times had he ridden a horse or used the toilet, with a three-second calculation, he would know the number. For his master to make such a statement about their sexual escapades brought Darcy more joy than he expected.

Pebb read all of this in his eyes and pulled Darcy close, pressing hot lips to his jaw. He said against Darcy's freshly-shaved cheek, "It is because you are so good at your work that you're leaving. Remember Oman?" Pebb chuckled, keeping his voice low so the men would know it was private. "You made such an impression on him that he sang your praises to the brethren in every settlement he traversed."

"I am honored," Darcy whispered.

It was time to depart and as Darcy had finally stopped growing, having topped out at 6'6", his master, at an inch shorter, physically lowered Darcy's head to kiss the crown.

"Go show Emil what my fix-it man can do."

"I will, Master," Darcy said and when released, he climbed beside the driver. The journey would be a long one and the night was only so many hours, but when he reached the Elder, life would begin again in many ways. A new master to study, to learn, to please and Darcy was up to the challenge.

Their journey was nearly complete when three months later, Darcy and his traveling companions stopped in a rowdy mortal pub for a round of drinks and diversion. His peculiar face and alluring posture drew attention from the humans they met. Male and female prostitutes offered their services a discount and the non-working lonelys also approached him seeking a sexual encounter. It was the group's leader, a captain named Fargo that shielded him from unwanted advances.

"We have a card game in back, Vandiver," Fargo said tonight when two women flanked Darcy at the bar. Fargo frightened them back with a fierce gaze and took Darcy by the bicep.

"Great timing," Darcy said and followed him down a dark hallway. "I'll make sure you're rewarded."

"Keep that reward to yourself, pup, I don't need fixing."

Darcy didn't believe him; they all needed fixing—even the ish-mikhan. Fargo fit in the category of the unwavering soldier— obeying without tilting left or right. With good humor, Darcy sent him an eyeroll and chose a seat among his brethren at a round table. A familiar tickle hummed behind his eye and he recognized the telepathic signature of a Rakum that had been contacting him intermittently his entire trek across the land. He opened his mind and the brother grasped his thread.

"My master wants to meet you. Don't leave the pub before we get there."

"I go where they take me, brother," Darcy returned as the man on his right dealt the cards. *"I am to be delivered to Elder Emil in a fortnight..."*

"Have you heard of Elder Kilmeade?" the brother asked.

Darcy began the hand to disguise his internal conversation. *"Of course,"* he sent back without an expression to those around him.

Kilmeade's name was on every Rakum's tongue the past few years. He'd developed an amazing reputation in the short time since his graduation. Some of the tales had to be rumors for they were much too outlandish to be true. The telepathic conversation did not resume and after another half-hour, it slipped his mind as the cards went his way.

Some hours later, Fargo snorted, a sound of surprise that carried no words, only an emotion of urgency. Every man felt it, translated via their conjoined telepathy, and when two of the brethren got to their feet, Darcy did too. He was about to ask what they were thinking when a new brother's face appeared in the doorway.

"I am Lucas Poppa. Which one of you is Darcy Vand—"

He didn't finish his telepathic query before an Elder stepped into view behind and over his left shoulder. Darcy did not need to be informed who it was—this master shined almost too brightly to see. It was Elder Kilmeade and Darcy's eyes squint in reaction to the light only ish-mikhan eyes discerned. Darcy's brethren dropped to the planked floor, prostrate and begging favor. Darcy had no such inclination. On the contrary, he couldn't look away from his master's gleaming countenance.

Poppa uttered introductions, but Darcy did not hear him. Every ounce of his concentration sought Kilmeade's pleasure, his mind sending a wordless sentiment of, *"whatever I have is yours, how can I serve you? You are perfect, beautiful, matchless…"*

The Elder met Darcy's eye, his expression lax. He stood 6'3", built strong and lean, with broad shoulders that sported a billowy black velvet cape. As the staring contest stretched on, the Elder put his fists to his hips and waited to see what Darcy would do.

"Bow, you shit! What's wrong with you?" one of his brothers hissed from the floor, but Darcy paid him no mind. Elder Kilmeade wanted him to do something… what did he want? It wasn't words...

What can I do to make that perfect master proud?

Then, as if just recalling his station, Darcy exhaled, stepped away from his brothers, around the table and toward the Elder. When he was three steps out, Kilmeade spun away and left the room. Darcy sent Poppa a thank you nod and followed the Elder into the boisterous pub.

Kilmeade walked through to the exit without pause or turning and then to a gleaming black carriage pulled by four Friesians blowing in the cold night air. Darcy did not think. A Rakum captain opened the carriage door; Darcy was five strides behind and when the Elder climbed smoothly into the blackness of the interior, Darcy followed without hesitation. He settled his weight across from Kilmeade and did not look away from the area of his face. The Elder barked commands to Poppa and the men outside. No one else boarded and the horses leapt forward.

With his heart racing, Darcy waited to see if his new master would speak. At that moment, in Rakum Hungarian, Kilmeade instructed Darcy to undress. He hadn't met his eye since the poker room, so in the minimum light of the interior, Darcy kept his eyes trained to the Elder's profile and removed his jacket and then the cotton smock. When his fingers went to his belt, Kilmeade swiveled his attention and watched him work it loose. Darcy was too tall to stand and he leaned forward preparing to slide off his trousers, but Kilmeade made a small noise in his throat he coupled with a tiny head shake. Then both hands fell to his lap, open and inviting. He lifted gray eyes, brighter than the moon, and Darcy fell into his master's gaze. Unable to stop himself, whimpered once as he went to his knees in the square of the carriage floor.

"What would you do now, Darcy?" the Elder asked and Darcy thought the master's voice would melt him entirely. He longed to hear another sentence, a word, anything, and he was unable to suppress a new moan when the master remained silent. Then Kilmeade smiled and his head tilted left, sending telepathically, *"Pass this test and I will talk your ear off."*

Darcy moved closer without hesitation. He knew what to do; an entire litany of things he could perform for his beloved master popped to mind and his training helped him choose which to use and in what order. By the time the carriage slowed at the first sun-up waystation, he had succeeded. Kilmeade kissed his mouth and began to speak. And Darcy listened, entranced, to every word.

Elder Kilmeade's Grand Experiment
Darcy Meets Jersey

The journey took two weeks, evenings spent in the carriage, flying across the ground, always pulled by fresh horses of the highest caliber. This Elder preferred luxury and so far, nothing they bought or ate was of less than superb quality. Each sun-up, they holed away in an established waystation, Kilmeade and Darcy in one room, the rest of the men scattered in the others. The Elder enjoyed Darcy's height and size, liked to lie beside and behind him, often snugged up tight for the few hours he slept. The Elder rose before Darcy every evening, his mind more advanced than any grunt's, but when they bedded down, the master wanted Darcy close. And Kilmeade would talk to him there in the dark, pressed together. He shared about his history, his adventures, his scientific explorations—anything that came to mind, the Elder would share, speaking low and romantically in Darcy's ear from behind.

The countryside rolled on with very few settlements or villages where a caravan could waylay, but Kilmeade demanded they patronize every opportunity, no matter how slight. On the fourth night of travel, the captain leading the train of six carriages and fourteen mounted Rakum soldiers trotted alongside and alerted Kilmeade of a home ahead where the farmer boarded travelers for a fee. The scout's nose had informed him that there was more than one female in residence so Kilmeade nodded they proceed. The Elder's carriage was center, so in turn, his driver halted before the door and a soldier opened the carriage for Kilmeade and Darcy to exit. Intuitively, Darcy positioned himself just behind the master's right shoulder once he noticed the lieutenant taking the left.

Watching every move the Elder made, Darcy noted his soldiers' behavior, too; none of them liked Darcy—not in the way he was accustomed. Their gazes were mere glances, too short for him to read. Before he pondered any further, his master said in his mind,

"Ignore them." Then Kilmeade shot him a mischievous wink. *"You are mine and they are safer pretending you disgust them. But they jerk off every sunup picturing your face."* The Elder mimed the movement with one hand at his crotch and giggled a silly sound Darcy had never heard in an adult Rakum. He rolled in his lips, mirroring his master's gleeful demeanor. This Elder was much more playful than Pebb and Darcy enjoyed it.

A few yards away, the farmer opened the wide door of his dwelling and strolled into the night, meeting them halfway down the grassy path. In Italian, he invited them to come inside, and with a wave of his hand, three young men less than fifteen jogged from behind the house to assume care of the horses. Darcy remained still as Kilmeade described what he required—a meal and some wine. The man introduced himself as Pavinni and gestured they enter. Kilmeade began forward and Darcy matched his movement, but the lieutenant remained back.

"I can't have that disgusting turd beside me amongst these mortals," Kilmeade sent to Darcy with humor. He gave him a cheery glance over his shoulder and resumed attending the farmer's idiot ramblings. *"Darcy Vandiver is all I need tonight."*

"You are correct, Master," Darcy returned with matching glee.

When the farmer led them into the house, both Rakum noticed three women in an adjacent kitchen, busily preparing savory-smelling dishes. Two were young and the other a matron of forty-five. Darcy did not turn, but in his peripheral vision, all three females watched them pass. To mortals, Elder Kilmeade would appear as young as Darcy—they would assume their guests to be not yet twenty—and they'd likely find him as attractive as the *ish-*

mikhan at his side. From the way they followed the pair with their eyes, Darcy figured he was right.

Pavinni sat them at a table, obviously his own when not serving travelers, and barked commands to the womenfolk out of sight. The maidens entered eyes averted, placed platters before them and disappeared again. Darcy grinned without intent, the beautiful sound of his master's increased heartrate bringing him joy.

"Begin choosing. We will eat this fine meal and then enjoy these people in whatever way pleases." Kilmeade's expression remained that of a stoic nobleman, but Darcy heard mixed in his transmission, *"choose who to drink and who to fuck."* So with care, he considered each as they consumed the meal.

Pavinni was short, overweight, and fifty, not in good health, and his skin had mottled with a speckled rash. Darcy doubted any of the Rakum would want him for anything. The three young boys were healthy and fine-looking, but his ears alerted him minutes ago that his brethren had already taken them to task in the barn. That left the mother and daughters.

"Who has cooked this delicious fare, *paisano*? I must meet her immediately and kiss her hand!" Kilmeade sang in Italian.

Pavinni called the women in and introduced them in order, wife, Syl, and daughters, Jules and Busella. Kilmeade remarked on how mature they behaved to be so young and the farmer graciously informed of their ages, twelve and fifteen this summer.

"Now, polcz-v', who will it be?" Kilmeade sent Darcy as the women bowed, politely looking aside and blushing.

Darcy was honest. *"I would drink the mother but bow to your will for the rest."*

Kilmeade raised his eyebrows. *"You can cause her to consent?"*

Darcy allowed his gaze to search out Syl's as he sent an answer to his master. *"I am positive I can get all of them to consent. You need only say the word."*

Kilmeade rose to his feet. "Pavinni, you and your family have made me very happy. Please go to the yard and bring in my driver. I want him to taste this delicious meal. He will pay you in gold. I hope that will suit."

The farmer smiled with rotten teeth and left them alone. The women would not hear the man's scream of surprise as the soldiers overtook him and Kilmeade turned to Darcy with a new grin.

"Ladies? Please, come close," Kilmeade said to the women waiting shyly along the wall. They advanced in tiny movements without meeting either man's eye.

"Tell me when, Master," Darcy sent, certain he would swoon the women within seconds. Kilmeade gave him a sideways wink, and Darcy took the hand of the closest woman. It was the younger daughter, Busella, and she looked up, craning her head to see into his face in the lamplight. Darcy laid it on thick—convincing her to give herself over, body and blood—and since she was a child, she saw him as an uncle or friend of her father's to be trusted and respected.

"Yes, Master," she said, her voice small and soft, "I consent."

Before her sister or mother reacted, Darcy tended them one at a time until all three verbally consented to whatever their guests might request.

"You are truly magnificent," Kilmeade said aloud and grasped the older daughter's hand. He walked her around the wall and Darcy remained. Syl and Busella watched them go and the mother turned.

"What can I get for you, honorable sir?" the woman asked in Italian, her accent that of the local agricultural community.

Darcy bent to her ear and whispered, "Show me to your sleeping quarters."

The woman glanced at her child and then left the room, Darcy directly behind. Busella did not follow and when they reached a small, dark room with a lumpy mattress and oil lamp set on the floor, Syl closed the door and flipped the drop-lock as soon as

Darcy entered. When she reached for her blouse strings Darcy covered her hand.

"I hunger for your blood," he whispered, his eyes hypnotizing all the while. She fell into his gaze and without reservation, delivered over her will. A female's consent caused the blood to take on an ambrosia-like quality and tonight because of Darcy's skill, he and Kilmeade would feast like kings. Darcy pulled free his knife and in a practiced movement the wound was made, and he lifted her up, Syl's feet off the floor. When he was finished, she was alive and unconscious. Darcy lay her onto the bed and left the room, seeking his master.

Elder Kilmeade had finished with the teen; he left her nude, unconscious, and bleeding. He came around the wall as Darcy reached him, brow raised with a question—*who did Darcy want to fuck?* Darcy parted his lips to answer and his master huffed.

"You prefer your brethren," he said as a statement and then clapped Darcy's shoulder hard. "You have a tremendous surprise coming, my pet. A gift so huge you won't believe your eyes."

Darcy's mouth formed a sideways grin at Kilmeade's sudden mysterious air. What in the world did he mean? In the current context, it would be a sexual gift. Darcy licked his lips, searching for the answer and his master squeezed his forearm.

"Focus, pet. The child, did you discern her illness?" he asked, looking up into Darcy's face.

Anew, Darcy was awed by his master's aura, everything about the Elder caused him distraction. He corralled his thoughts before Kilmeade reacted and answered with a shake of the head. Darcy was a healer, but not a true diagnostician.

"Consumption. She'll live another year," his master said and turned for the exit. "We will leave her with her mother and sister. Our brethren may yet pass by here in the next few months and I will leave word of consenting females in this place."

Darcy nodded as he followed him out. Their brethren had readied the horses and loaded the other carriages. Kilmeade climbed into their vehicle and Darcy followed, the master's personal scent mixing now with that of the female he'd bedded.

Was he satisfied? Darcy did not invite the idiotic questions that tickled his mind, but that didn't prevent them from assaulting him as the horses kicked off. *Does he prefer a female's attentions? Am I not enough?*

Kilmeade's piercing gaze finally broke his internal monologue with its power. Darcy met his eye in the dark space, his master licking his lips and then slowly tipping his chin to the side.

"A mortal…" Kilmeade began in their language and then fell into telepathy to finish. "*…a human is beneath me, beneath you…*" He forced a shiver. "*…Beneath every brother in our population. I hate them. I loathe them all. I see them as dirty, roach-like, and simple-minded. But…*"

He paused and summoned Darcy closer with two fingers. Darcy dropped to the carriage floor onto his knees and sat upon his rump his face tilted upward.

"Like a roach, they are useful. They maintain our planet," he said in his silky voice, switching to Italian, Darcy's favorite when spoken by his master. "Both sexes have hands to work and soft places to release our lust." He shrugged. "I will always prefer my kind over them. As you age, you will find no Rakum truly favors a mortal. Mark my word."

And Darcy did—he listened and memorized it all.

Finally, the entourage had reached the last evening's ride which would bring them to Kilmeade's Italian estate. Minutes before sundown in the waystation safe place, Darcy rose to don his clothing but Kilmeade bade he wait, addressing him from a nearby chair.

"Let me look upon you in this light." With his chin to the side, Kilmeade moved the oil lamp across Darcy's body. "Oh, yes. Your appearance is resplendent! How did you escape my awareness for more than six decades?"

Darcy watched his eyes. The question had been rhetorical and he awaited more. Knowing his master found him so overwhelming to the senses gave him immense pleasure and he wished with every fiber of his being that he could somehow repay him for all he had done and would do in the future.

"You serve me, Darcy, that is your payment and my reward. Isn't this a beautiful marriage of master and ish-mikhan!"

Again, Darcy remained mute, but he flexed his muscles in such a way that Kilmeade smiled and wrinkled his nose.

"Oh, my precious pet! It is nearly time. As promised, I saved the best surprise for last," he said, a twinkle of mischief in his bright gray eyes. "I have another *ish-mikhan*."

Darcy's jaw dropped. He had not met any of his kind and his master nodded at the excitement building in his servant.

"Yes, my first pup, his name is Jersey, and it is my will that the two of you will be companions. You will be compatible and ply your skills together, with each other, and apart. This experiment will be my top priority until I am satisfied that I have learned all I can."

His master's grin widened as Darcy worked to imagine what another fix-it man might be like. And what they would do together, and what power their coupling might introduce to the world. He tried to see his counterpart's face in his master's mind, but Kilmeade blocked him, explaining it was part of the experiment. With eager expectation, Darcy dressed under his master's watchful eye and awaited their departure.

In two hours, the carriage pulled to the gigantic double door of a huge stone wall. This was the castle's outer gate, and once opened, the horses carried them another hundred yards to the house entrance. Darcy stepped down from the carriage and Kilmeade followed directly after. He touched his elbow and Darcy turned.

"Stand here. I must see your faces at the meet. Close your eyes; Pluto will lead you forward when I call."

Darcy closed his eyes with a tight grin, his heart hammering. He absorbed the sounds of the brethren nearby and, their body scents, and that of the livestock and a hearty stew cooking in the house. Pluto took his bicep in hand and tugged him forward. Darcy stepped from gravel to smooth stone and walked twenty-five paces, gruffly led by the arm. A new body scent reached his nostrils; it was the ish-mikhan. He smelled of lavender soap and something else, something close to Darcy's own aroma, pheromones and excited perspiration. Kilmeade was nearby and Darcy waited for the command to open his eyes. He and the other ish-mikhan were placed barely three feet apart—he felt the man's body heat now—and Kilmeade stood to his left forming a three-man triangle.

He heard in his mind, *"Open your eyes."*

"Darcy Vandiver, meet Jersey. My first pup."

Oh...

Darcy's inhale had been audible. Jersey stepped into him, craning his neck in an exaggerated movement, grinning wide at their height difference. Darcy looked down on him, the most beautiful Rakum he had ever seen—green eyes, emerald and shining, hair soft, wavy, and nearly the same color as his own, a strong build of balance and allure. It seemed much more than he deserved and as the thought tickled his inner mind, Jersey's eye twinkled. He lifted warm palms to either side of Darcy's face, cupping gently and diving deep into his gaze. Darcy remained immobile in his grasp, seeing in Jersey's face a future brighter than the sun.

"He's a romantic, Master," Jersey said then, looking into Darcy's eyes but speaking to Kilmeade. "He is perfect. You honor me with this magnificent companion."

Still speechless, Darcy moistened his lips.

"You are home," Jersey sent, reading him more easily than

any grunt ever had. Then Jersey applied the tiniest bit of pressure to Darcy's cheeks in case he wanted to lean down. *"Ish-mikhan don't need words, do we?"*

Darcy bent down, his head rushing.

"It is our master's will that we be compatible," Jersey said in a soft voice that flowed with substance to Darcy's ears. "Do you think we can do that?" he asked even smoother.

In drawing him into the house, Pluto had led him into a bedroom, Darcy only now aware of the enormous soft-mattressed bed to his right. With his head and groin pounding with blood, he cupped Jersey's neck with one big hand and pulled him close. At first, he smashed their lips together, closed-mouthed and sealed tight. One, two, three seconds he held Jersey fiercely to his own face. Then, when he relaxed the pressure to the man's neck, the kiss opened and Darcy dove in, withholding nothing.

Jersey chuckled, still connected, his breath filling Darcy's cheeks. Darcy recognized the sound—it was joy. He felt it, too. The embrace morphed into explorations, the difference in their heights no challenge as Darcy's right hand caressed Jersey's chest and at his middle, Jersey worked loose his belt. Darcy ripped his mouth from Jersey's with a smack, feeling his own grin and seeing it reflected in his companion's shining face. With a violent shove, he pushed Jersey onto the bed and hopped upon him in a straddle as the world and their audience melted into his subconscious.

Darcy propped his weight upon open hands at either side of Jersey's head. *"What will you teach me, Master?"* he sent telepathically, respecting Jersey's seniority.

"Wonderful things," Jersey returned, their eyes locked, his knees coming up to Darcy's lower back. *"So many wonderful things."*

With another joyful chuckle from them both, the two ish-mikhan found themselves more compatible than they could ever have imagined. And Kilmeade was pleased.

Kilmeade's Greatness
Too Bad for Yu

Year 1785

"Elder Yu? Here?" (pause) "Where is Master Kilmeade?"

Darcy's deep voice jostled Jersey from sleep. They had been keeping odd hours the past two weeks as Elder Kilmeade rotated his fellow Elders through the estate. Officially, they were attending business of the Fathers; unofficially, Jersey's master was showing off his dual fix-it men.

"Jerz, come on," Darcy said closer.

Still groggy, Jersey opened his eyes. In the back of his mind, a feather tickled as the unfamiliar Elder approached. He'd learned early on that when the Elders were near, his subconscious knew before his natural senses. Jersey attempted to rise, but his brain longed to sleep. He allowed a soft moan and succumbed, slipping back to the covers. The next sensation he knew was being violently jerked from his bed. Without a word or vocal admonishment, Jersey was shaken so furiously that his head swam. When he opened his eyes, he stared directly into Elder Yu's snarling face.

"Master!" Jersey focused, bringing his body online. Yu was incensed, his ire directed wholly to the man in his vicious grip. In the periphery, Darcy stood at attention, soldier-style, lined up with Kilmeade's captains, but Jersey did not look away from the Elder's red gaze. "I am your servant; whatever I have is yours," he rasped, aware he was moments away from severe punishment, his behavior greatly offending his master.

Yu was glorious and no other word—in any language—could possibly describe him. He towered over any man in the room, even Darcy, and if his height wasn't enough, his presence filled Jersey's consciousness as if not another person existed but himself and the god holding him inches off the ground.

"Oh, if I could please him, if only I could make him proud," Jersey's heart cried out, the interior workings of the Rakum unafraid of pain and the ish-mikhan spirit unafraid of appearing weak.

Yu lifted him over his head, spun him 180-degrees to drop him hard to the stone floor, Jersey's upper back absorbing the concussion with a snap of his scapula. The pain registered as a miniscule distraction as his vision cleared and he sought another view of Yu's face, now in profile as he shouted commands to the others in Rakum Hungarian.

"Oh, you are perfect, and I will show you… I am able to make you smile…" Jersey's heart continued to sing the Elder's praises and he lay still, his fractured bones healing with an itching tug. Yu swiveled his gaze and locked black eyes with Jersey's, still incensed.

He's angry with Kilmeade.

Jersey was unable to stop such thoughts, which trickled into his mind because of his predisposition to serve Elders. None of this eased Yu's hotly directed fury.

"If you like my thoughts so very much, have this one!" he barked in their language, bending low and because of his sheer size, appearing as if he moved in half-time to grasp Jersey about the throat. Jersey saw in his mind that the Elder wished him broken, *utterly.*

Kilmeade has stolen away his mate.

Another intuited thought slipped by and then—

No, she left Yu in preference to Kilmeade.

"Enough!" the master barked aloud and in his mind. Yu then shoved Jersey's body against the stone wall with all his might.

Jersey's vision blurred and he blinked out.

When he swam back, warm hands, supportive and healing, covered his wounds. He had only been out a few seconds. Elder

Yu stood over him, seething, but Darcy was now at Jersey's side, his aroma as familiar as Jersey's own. His compatriot touched his cheeks with both hands—

Wait... then who's healing me?

Jersey lifted his gaze and over his left shoulder, he caught a tiny glimpse of auburn hair, soft waves that fluttered out of view, his master furiously repairing what Yu had broken. Kilmeade was in the habit of suppressing his body scent and in the melee Jersey had forgotten. Within another minute, every injury had been repaired and Kilmeade tenderly lifted Jersey to his feet.

"Elder Yu." Kilmeade spoke the name in a stern but quiet tone. "Welcome to my home." Jersey avoided Yu's eye recognizing that Kilmeade was reprimanding his fellow Elder. "Leave us," he continued in the same voice. "Ish-mikhan, remain."

The grunts and soldiers of both masters filed out. Darcy stood and moved to the wall near the door, awaiting a command, his eyes cast aside. Kilmeade's hands cupped Jersey's shoulders from behind and he ran one palm to his throat and stroked tenderly.

"You make me so proud," he sent privately and kissed the back of his ear with soft lips. To their guest, Kilmeade said in their language, "How do you find my ish-mikhan? Hardy, isn't he?"

It had been more a statement than a question and Jersey peeked for the Elder's response. His eyebrow fluttered, his lip curled, and then he relaxed his shoulders. Kilmeade had perhaps been speaking to Yu privately and Jersey pretended he didn't notice. Of course, both Elders caught his sentiment.

"Darcy," Kilmeade said, "show Master Yu to his quarters."

Jersey sighed and tried to hide it. Yu would prefer Darcy anyway—he was huge and just as capable of fixing the convolutions that ruined the Elder's mood tonight.

The two exited without a word or glance and when they were gone, Kilmeade turned Jersey in his grasp.

"You are an amazing seer, my pet, but you missed with Elder Yu." Kilmeade's gray eyes shone with affection and he kissed

Jersey's mouth, hot and lingering. Jersey's respirations hyped, prepared to switch on and Kilmeade pulled back to see his face. "Yes, I took Yu's mate, but no, he doesn't prefer Darcy over you."

Jersey wondered at his words and Kilmeade kissed him again, sending silently, *"He raced me here tonight, sabotaged my mount so I had to run on foot. He wanted to ravish you and I forbid it. The best he could do before I arrived was break you a little…"*

"But he doesn't have to resist—if he wants me dead even, his will—" Jersey said in a low voice.

Kilmeade cut him off. *"No one does anything against what is mine. I allowed him to break you—as payback for little Jasmine, but none of them can best me in any capacity."*

Jersey said nothing. He had decided years ago that Kilmeade was their greatest Elder. Apparently, a goliath such as Yu recognized the same thing.

"Let him fuck Darcy. He does not deserve you—Kilmeade's first pup." Kilmeade gave him a devilish smile. *"Never forget your status. This title will follow you your entire life. You have earned it and you will always be my beloved favorite pet."*

Several rooms away, in the direction of the guest quarters, a loud crash sounded, reverberating the wall, before the house fell silent.

Kilmeade tweaked one eyebrow and then showed Jersey his pointer finger. *"Wait for it…"* he sent, his eyes to the side and sounds of pleasure followed. "Yu is fixed," he said aloud and dropped his hands to cross them at his chest. "Now, I have an itch."

"I will scratch it for you, Master," Jersey said low and Kilmeade grinned.

Jersey Meets Master Brandon

Kilmeade, Triple Badass

Year 1810

Tonight, the Rakum brotherhood had been summoned to gather for a status check. In the main building, Jersey hugged the wall and looked away when Elder Kilmeade's entourage passed. His time with the Elder had ended and it did him no good to presume he remained in favor. When he raised his eyes, the last man had slowed and stopped to shoot him a sly grin.

"Why are you hiding, little girl?" he asked, and Jersey checked the Elder's distance away before responding with a smile of his own.

"Kazak, Darss. It's been too long. You look well."

Darcy Vandiver encircled Jersey's neck with huge hands and pulled him close. Instead of bumping foreheads, he stooped his 6'6" frame to touch their mouths. Five long seconds they kissed, Darcy's lips butter soft. His brother ended the move by grabbing Jersey's lower lip with his teeth. When he stood to press his face into Jersey's hair, he chuckled a low sound.

"You don't smell right," he said, the words muffled. "You aren't getting enough head."

"Is that an offer?" Jersey replied and prepared to respond with his body. Then his friend sighed. "What's up?"

"Kilmeade is handing me off," Darcy said low and leaned out. "You look different."

71

Jersey huffed. "Elder Fawn assigned me to his soldiers in Mexico." Jersey met Darcy's eye; as ish-mikhan, he'd been instructed to keep the company stress-free, which Jersey enjoyed, but the place itself, the residence provided, the entire *country* left much to be desired in the way of comfort and luxury. He shivered in disgust and Darcy chuckled.

"Spoiled baby," Darcy replied in a grin.

"I am what I am," Jersey said in an approximation of Master Kilmeade's voice. "Where will you go?"

Darcy parted his lips but stopped as a strong hand grasped his shoulder. Jersey saw who it was lowered his eyes.

"Master, kazak, you look well," he whispered.

"Slinking around in the shadows," the Elder teased, his dramatic gray eyes twinkling. Darcy stepped sideways and Kilmeade filled the space. "Are you avoiding your favorite Elder?"

"Yes, Master." The Elder had a new ish-mikhan and had sent Jersey away. The Elder scoffed at his thoughts and cupped Jersey's neck with both palms.

"You know better than that," he sent telepathically, and his eyes fell to Jersey's shirtfront. With an inhale of disgust, he slid his contact down Jersey's arms to end at his fingers. "Why are you dressed this way?" he asked lifting apart their joined hands.

With lowered eyes, Jersey considered his attire. Elder Fawn allowed him no money so he wore whatever he could find, steal, or borrow. Before he answered, the Elder shook his head, a spark of anger kindled in his gaze.

"Elder Fawn doesn't favor him," Darcy offered.

Kilmeade's eyes narrowed. "Is this how you would characterize Master Fawn?"

Jersey stuck to the truth. "Yes."

A twitch in the Elder's cheek revealed an internal conversation underway. The Elder then brought Jersey's hands to his lips. *"This will not do,"* he sent silently.

A heavy footfall approached and two enormous dark-brown hands landed on Darcy's outer shoulders. "Darcy Vandiver, welcome to my pack," a growly voice boomed.

Kilmeade dropped Jersey's hands to address Elder Bel. With undisguised warning, he said, "Brother, you will do well to remember this Rakum is favored."

"Shit, I favor him already. He's magnificent." The large Black Rakum ran one hand through Darcy's long hair and grasped it in his fist. "Shit! You're built like an Elder." Bel's free hand roamed Darcy's pecs, squeezed his bicep, and laughed. "Do you fight?"

With his head forced back, Darcy answered in a near-normal voice, "Indeed, Master."

Bel released him and their eyes met. Three long seconds ticked by as Bel stared into Darcy's face. Then, a slow smile partnered with a low chuckle issued from the giant Elder's chest. *"Fuck me, this is a great night!"* Bel locked his hand around the back of Darcy's neck. "Come, little brother, let us begin."

Quietly and side-by-side, Kilmeade and Jersey watched them walk away. After another moment, the Elder faced Jersey with a *tsk.*

"Of all my pups, your cognitive acuity exceeds expectations. Tell me why I send my ish-mikhan away."

Jersey absorbed the compliment aware his lazy reasoning had offended his master. "It is for our sake," Jersey said, holding Kilmeade's educating glare. "We grow too attached. It leads to weakness."

The Elder's grin widened and after another long moment studying Jersey's face, he clucked his tongue—topic closed. He then turned away, walking fast and Jersey followed to the Elder's assigned room.

They had been in the apartment only a minute when another Elder entered the still-open door. This was Elder Brandon, whom Jersey had seen at a distance, but never met. He nodded and the comely Elder returned the gesture. He acknowledged Kilmeade, crossed his arms, and tucked his chin to the side as if listening telepathically. Jersey waited, studying his appearance. Brandon was Jersey's height with wavy black hair and a trimmed beard. His green eyes sparkled with anticipation and he again eyed Jersey with approval when finished speaking privately. As the three of them looked each other over, Elder Fawn entered, his mouth set in a frown. In keeping with protocol, Jersey made as if to cross to him, but Kilmeade telepathically commanded him to remain in place.

"Shit, Kilmeade! You cannot *summon* me!" the Elder barked. "And what's wrong with you, asshole?" he said when Jersey met his eye. "COME CLOSE!"

Kilmeade made a noise in his throat and Fawn inhaled, jerking his gaze to the other Elders.

"Are you ready?" Kilmeade asked in a soft voice.

"The audacity!" Fawn began, his voice decidedly less edgy than before. Kilmeade's audible sigh silenced him.

"Will you hear it?" he asked in a bored monotone. One hand reached for the lapel of Jersey's dingy coat and pulled him close. He wrapped that arm about Jersey's shoulders, his eyes on Fawn.

Jersey's master exhaled with an angry snort and his gaze glittered with fury. When Kilmeade made another grumble deep down, Fawn screamed, "YES! Shit! Go ahead! Do your worst!"

Kilmeade said in an undertone, "Excommunicated."

Fawn inhaled in shock. "Where? How long?"

"How long have you disdained my favored one?"

Fawn looked to Brandon for help. Jersey knew the sentence down to the minute and he recounted the number in his mind, watching Fawn's mouth. Finally, the accused dropped his eyes.

"Six years, seven months, two days," he groused and looked hard at Jersey. Kilmeade stepped between them and put one hand to Fawn's throat.

"Six years, seven months, two days shall you be in exile. The Yukon—anywhere in the region is fine, but your travel is not part of your sentence. Get there quickly."

"Kilmeade," Fawn countered deflating until inaudible.

Kilmeade waved his fingers and after another moment, the angry Elder stomped out. Kilmeade maneuvered Jersey until he stood inches from his face. "Use my shower. When you have washed, dress in my finest clothing and rejoin us. Go now."

Jersey allowed a small grin and turned for the bathroom. Unlike the grunt's communal situation with water nightly carried in from outdoors, the Elder's tiled shower boasted indoor plumbing heated by a coal furnace. Jersey took longer than necessary, possibly testing Kilmeade's patience, but the reward of the hot water and the silky lather of the imported French soaps seemed worth the risk of chastisement. After toweling off, he strolled the length of his master's closet. He and Kilmeade were similar in size and he gamely selected the most expensive costume in the Elder's collection. Complete with polished ash walking cane, Jersey re-joined his masters.

"My beautiful pet!" Kilmeade announced, his striking features alive with cheer. "I knew you were still in there!"

"This is proper attire for Kilmeade's first pup," Brandon agreed with a loud clap of his hands.

Kilmeade met Jersey across the floor. "Brandon will favor you," he told him, caressing his cheek and then turning to the other Elder. "Jersey is clever, funny as hell, and serves eagerly."

"I can see all that at a glance," Brandon said, his tone playful. Jersey didn't grin, but his eyes may have, for Brandon scrunched his nose and jabbed Kilmeade's shoulder. "Hand him over, brother. I'm ready to explore his talents." Brandon shouldered Kilmeade to the side and draped one arm across Jersey's lower back. "He is wickedly handsome."

Jersey offered the phrase all Elders love. "Your will is my will."

Brandon turned enough to shove Jersey toward the door. "It is good to be the master!"

"Jersey," Kilmeade called in a quiet tone. "Show Elder Brandon why, for the rest of my life, you will be remembered as my favorite."

Brandon hummed with a low chuckle. "*Shi-i-i-t!* Let us depart!" Pulling Jersey from the suite, Brandon called his other grunts from where they had been waiting. A five-minute walk under a full moon across the expansive grounds and they reached the Elders' apartments. Once inside, Brandon introduced Jersey. These were the soldiers with which he traveled and each welcomed Jersey with sincerity.

"Listen well, Jersey is for me. Keep your fucking dicks to yourself," the Elder announced. "Now, leave us." The brethren exited remarking openly to each other regarding their Elder's new addition. Brandon watched Jersey with his fists to his hips. "You will be my first ish-mikhan. How do we begin?"

Jersey's lips parted and he paused at the humble statement, discerning this Elder differed from the others he had served. Brandon would give his favored-one leniency and as the thought crossed Jersey's mind, Brandon scrunched his nose.

"Reading me already?" The Elder crossed muscled arms at his chest and lowered his chin. "I like you in my head, I'm hard as a rock since our eyes met."

Jersey pressed his lips closed; there was no reply to such a statement from a master. Elders kept sentiments of that ilk to themselves and as he considered that, Brandon lowered his chin.

"I do what I want. I say what I want. I fuck who I want." Brandon's eye twinkled and Jersey saw in his mind something he must have misread—*Brandon wonders what it's like to catch…*

"Hah! Beautiful *polcz-v'!*" Brandon's eyes flicked to the bolted door and back to his face. "Kilmeade has taught you wonderful things which I will exploit, but he has held you at arm's length. *I intend to pull you all the way in…*"

Brandon had sent the last sentiment telepathically and Jersey's eyes widened; even his new master's mental voice flowed differently across his psyche—exciting and a little dangerous.

Brandon smiled. "You will show me even greater things than you've ever shown another Elder. I have been weary and bored for a decade." The Elder closed his mouth and sent silently, *"I am certain with you, I will expand my knowledge."*

Jersey pondered his statement, flattered and awaiting a nudge from his instincts. His internal muse gave him a phrase—not spoken, but felt, and he released it. The emotion he transferred said, *"I will blow your mind."*

Brandon laughed aloud and took the last step into Jersey's space. *"What am I thinking now?"* he sent silently.

All grunts could read their masters' surface thoughts, but none of them would. An ish-mikhan got away with it since the master's desires were the fix-it man's entire world. Jersey read that Brandon wanted to be studied, experimented on, and to be the focus of his full attention. Lastly, his most urgent need—the Elder wanted Jersey's eye.

"Show me the look," he said, suddenly breathy.

With a playful sideways grin, Jersey averted his attention to the fireplace.

"Jersey," Brandon breathed and inched closer, "that was a command."

Jersey sucked his teeth, sighed for effect, and swiveled his face to his new master. The Elder did not resist, allowing the physiological effects of the magnetic eye contact to blossom across his frame. Blood rushed to his cheeks, limbs, and lower, and a wide smile erupted on his handsome face.

"I will never release you," [12]the Elder sent silently and lifted both hands to Jersey's cheeks to pull him close. With nothing appropriate to remark, Jersey allowed a small grin and began the evening.

---

[12] *(In honor of this great master, I will attest that he held me until Last Assembly, two-hundred years. He is well-missed. ~Jersey)*

Elder Canaan's Kryptonite

Darcy Woos Elder Canaan

Year 1931

Sent by Father Umbarto, three grunts arrived one starless October night to Canaan's residence. Tork, Canaan's lieutenant, had them wait in the foyer while he awaited his master's command. Usually a somber sort, Tork was inexplicably amused.

Canaan grinned by reflex. *"What the fuck?"* he sent silently.

"One of these guys," Tork began and shook his head to chuckle. *"Father Umbarto must think you're lonely."*

"What are you getting at?" Canaan responded, laughing with him. The man didn't reply and Canaan smirked. "Send them in, idiot," he said aloud and resumed a serious expression. With a curt nod, Tork turned and left the room.

He directed the men and Canaan observed each as he entered. When the third came into view, he understood his lieutenant's reaction. The Father had sent a fix-it man, a fucking statue of perfection who exuded masculinity, owning it with a swagger that incorporated every cell. As Canaan pondered number three's appearance, the senior grunt began the introductions.

"Master Canaan, I am Yan," the first man said. "This is Ken, and in the back is Darcy Vandiver. We will serve your will."

Canaan regarded the leader, forcing his eyes away from the third grunt with determination. Yan and Ken were strong, sturdy

78

types, both Asian with striking features and shimmering black hair past their shoulders. All three men wore suits, but number three had removed his coat and rolled up his sleeves. Even peripherally, Canaan noticed his defined and deeply tanned forearms, never mind that Rakum never absorbed UV after graduation from First Ritual.

Finally weary of his self-induced consternation, Canaan looked Yan in the eye. "Go find Tork." He flicked his eyes to the third man. "Vandiver, you stay."

The shit grinned and crossed his arms with a friendly smile that caused Canaan's dick to jump. Vandiver's eyes were bizarre—yellowy-hazel; Canaan had never seen the like. Add to that, the man *used* them, attempting to manipulate Canaan from the initial eye-meet. Ish-mikhan did that, Canaan expected it, but he did not expect his blood pressure to head up and his breath-rate increase.

"Step up," Canaan instructed not disguising his amusement. Vandiver obediently complied to stop within arm's reach. He held Canaan's gaze with a new smile, tiny and to the side. The grunt's ethereal fingers reached for Canaan's thread and stroked, reading anything Canaan left on the front porch. He allowed it, holding the man's gaze, aware the man would see his attraction.

"Master, you are beautiful," the grunt sent, his telepathic voice nearly bringing Canaan to climax. With a loud laugh, Canaan lowered his eye and wrapped one hand around the Rakum's throat.

"Shut the fuck up, asshole," Canaan laugh-talked and looked inside. Vandiver's thread stood prominent and he grasped it, hoping to divine something of the man's history. *"Show me your last assignment."*

In the grunt's memory and through his perspective, Canaan watched Tomás approach, ask Vandiver a few questions, and walk away entirely unaffected by the pup's magnetism.

Canaan wiggled the Rakum's neck. "Did it hurt your feelings, little brother, that Tomás would rather eat shit than spend another second in your presence?"

"Yes, Master," the Rakum responded with levity, his deep and rolling voice much too soothing. "I cry myself to sleep every sunrise."

Canaan lifted his gaze. The pup was ballsy and irreverent and might have been baiting Canaan to attack him. As the thought entered his mind, Vandiver's lips rolled in restraining a grin. Without further thought, Canaan dropped the contact and viciously clocked the guy's jaw with a right hook. Vandiver's mass launched backward, landing on the long sofa. Canaan stood over him prepared to administer a second blow when the Rakum relaxed his posture to appear as if he was merely reclining.

"Powerful, Master. Simply amazing," Vandiver said holding Canaan's gaze. When Canaan paused, simply to enjoy the sight, Vandiver licked his lips in slow motion and arched his brows. "Please, let's do that once more."

"Narcissistic asshole son-of-a-bitch," Canaan said with a wry grin and reached down to grasp his expensive shirt by both lapels. With an urgent movement meant to yank the man off the couch, the cotton ripped. Canaan held the tattered garment in his hands, a grin tickling his mouth. Now the beautiful brother was topless. Canaan's eyes drank in the new man's physique as if he had been thirsting forever. Although surrounded by soldiers he had handpicked over the years, he never saw any of them as he was envisioning Darcy Vandiver. Something about the ish-mikhan exceeded the norm and Canaan urgently needed to dig it out. The grunt saw all this in Canaan's mind and grinned.

"Fuck," Canaan whispered and smiled as well. "Say it," he grunted, happy they were alone and he wouldn't have to smash his captains for witnessing his arousal. Slowly and with intent, Vandiver raised both arms to prop his head in his hands.

"Whatever I have is yours," the man said, his voice melodious.

With a release of pent sexual tension, Canaan laughed and

pointed to the hallway. "Last room on the right, asshole."

Still clutching the man's shredded dress shirt in his fist, Canaan watched Vandiver tumble from the couch with humorous drama and turn for the hall. Behind him Tork entered and cleared his throat. Canaan didn't turn, his eyes on the ish-mikhan's back.

"So, my master is happy?" Tork sent, probably enjoying himself too much at Canaan's expense.

"Do not disturb," Canaan whispered and headed for his quarters.

❖

12 weeks later

"Your master will arrive within the hour," Canaan said, comfortable and reflecting on the past several weeks.

Without responding, Darcy Vandiver got to his feet and handed over Canaan's slacks. He read that the grunt thought to head for the bath and Canaan shook his head.

"No shower," he added with a mischievous grin that garnered no reaction from his guest. Canaan wasn't much of an explainer, so he left it alone. Stepping into his pants, he watched Vanny dress and then weave a leather belt into his slacks. Before he remarked on the show, Elder Bel's voice in his head caused him to chuckle.

"I hope your dick rotted off," his compatriot teased in a deep telepathic vibrato. *"I'm coming up. You will hand over my lieutenant. Enough of this shit."*

Canaan had stepped close as he listened to Bel and he motioned for Vanny to leave his white dress shirt open. With one hand to the man's abdomen, fuzzy with cinnamon-brown hair, Canaan absorbed his warmth. He related Bel's private telepathic remarks and Vanny's mouth made the tiniest grin before he raised his eyes to lock with Canaan's. Being ish-mikhan was only a fraction of the attraction—the metaphysical reaction needed to be investigated and Canaan would not rest until he figured it out.

"An Elder must always be learning," so, Canaan worked the guy over in every way he could imagine, digging into his deepest inward parts. Some of his explorations were physical, but just as many were done fully-clothed, all for the purpose of divining the origination of the unique hold Darcy had on Canaan's imagination.

Needles pricked Canaan's inner mind; the grunt had questions that he wasn't sure he should voice. Canaan didn't have to read him; *"Can I stay with you?"* was written all over the man's flawless face.

Downstairs, Bel entered the apartment barking orders to Canaan's men. With one last thoughtful pass across Vanny's muscular midriff, the man began buttoning up.

"If you want him so badly, come get him," Canaan sent and turned to watch the bedroom door. When the Elder pushed into the room, Canaan assumed a wide grin.

Bel didn't look at him. Instead, he eyed Vanny who crossed without hesitation. Ebony-skinned, Bel was built wide across the shoulders and stood 6'7"; an inch taller than Vanny and three inches taller than Canaan. He placed a huge hand to Vanny's neck and pulled him close, burying his nose in the man's long hair. Canaan snickered, knowing what was coming. Looking up from the grunt's head, he caught Canaan's eye.

"Fuck, Canaan! You fed him your blood?"

Canaan nodded rapidly, really grinning. Vanny would smell like Canaan for being around so long, for sleeping in his bed, and for wearing his clothing during their visit, but consuming an Elder's blood would cause a scent transfer that would linger for weeks. Bel was aged and serious; seeing him grow angrier was supremely entertaining. Canaan finally laughed out loud in one huge burst and Bel narrowed his eyes.

After a long stream of profanity, Bel called for Canaan's lieutenant at the top of his lungs. Tork jogged in at attention. With no explanation to the surprised inferior, Bel dropped contact with Darcy Vandiver and shoved a quickly-produced knife-blade to his own inner arm. He grabbed Tork and forced his face to the wound. Canaan's top man pulled the blood without touching the Elder except with his mouth and when Bel shoved him off his arm, Tork backed to the wall and waited for the next edict.

Smiling, Canaan motioned for Tork to step up and he sniffed the man's dark blond hair. "Oh, so delightful," Canaan cooed. He didn't care what his soldiers smelled like—he didn't fuck them. After another moment, Bel sent them out and Tork pulled the bedroom door as the last to exit. The room fell still and Bel lifted one hand to drop onto Vanny's near shoulder in a gentle massage.

"I see what you're doing," Bel sent privately, his massaging hand growing still. *"Before I leave, I'm still going to fuck you up."*

"I hope so," Canaan said aloud and Bel sucked his teeth.

"Darcy wants to know why he can't remain with you," Bel said, watching Canaan's face. "Come close, Elder. Let us educate our little brother."

Canaan stepped into their space and sent Vanny a comforting grin. Bel opened the hand on Vanny's shoulder and went into the man's long hair.

"First, explain to Darcy why he's with me and not you." As his superior, Bel chose to test Canaan, to see if he fully understood the reasoning behind Vanny's placement.

Canaan discerned all this and said to the grunt, "You like me too much." Vanny met his gaze. "Affinity is fine, camaraderie is good, but infatuation?" Canaan shook his head. "Your masters won't allow you to fall into weakness. *Comprende?*"

Vanny did not reply and his eyes narrowed. Canaan waited to read the man's impressions. Vanny's surface thoughts trickled over; he didn't see the problem. Canaan flicked his eyes to Bel who bade him continue the lesson. Canaan brought up one hand to cup Vanny's strong shoulder.

"Group lair, you became too attached to your proctor. Later, you became too fond of your first Elder. You were selected by Kilmeade and became too fond of him. There's a brother—

Jersey—you are also too chummy with. Up to this point, am I on target?" Canaan asked and Vanny agreed with a slow nod. "Consider Elder Bel and Elder Canaan. Do you feel the same way about us?"

Vanny's gaze darted between them and he slowly shook his head. Canaan felt done, but Bel wanted him to continue. Wondering what might fall past his lips, Canaan barreled on, trusting his instincts as he'd been trained.

"You are a powerful Rakum. If you grow too attached to anyone other than yourself, you will lose some of that power. Affection is *human.* Need I say more?" Canaan held Vanny's gaze. After a moment he blinked and turned to meet Bel's eye.

"I do not wish to be weak," he said in his distinct smooth voice. "I thank you for this lesson."

Bel humphed and shot his gaze to Canaan. "Did you see that?" he asked and Canaan grinned. The grunt had posed a silent question inside the spoken one—*"does Master Canaan feel the same way about me?"*

Canaan shook his head and Bel poked him mentally. *"Finish it."*

"All of your masters are scholars, scientists, digging for answers to anything we don't yet know," he said low as Vanny turned to sink his yellowy-brown eyes into Canaan's. "This..." With his left hand, Canaan unbuttoned the top several inches of Vanny's shirt and pressed his palm to the man's bare upper chest. "Look at my hand." Canaan waited and the grunt did as instructed. "Now see it with your eyes closed."

Without hesitation, Vanny dropped his lids. The average brother did not learn this trick, but the smart ones could pick it up. Canaan waited while the man's keen mind focused on rebuilding the image. When he had a firm recollection, Canaan continued the lesson.

"I want you to see the electricity between us—the palm of my hand and the surface of your skin. Look for sparks and what will appear to be lightning bouncing between us." Canaan became aware of Bel boosting the grunt's mental acuity with a finger to the man's neck. Vanny visualized the energy and made a noise in his throat. "Now, keeping your eyes closed, watch my hand," Canaan said and slowly removed his palm to travel toward Bel, who opened his shirt the same measure. Vanny kept his eyes closed, but his head tilt indicated he yet followed Canaan's movement without optics. Canaan pressed his palm to Bel's deep brown skin and waited for Vanny's remarks. No electricity passed between them and when Canaan noted Bel's eye in his periphery, the huge Elder grinned with approval.

"Master, you want me to see that your body and mine have a physical reaction to one another that is unique, perhaps rare. Is this correct?" Vanny asked, eyes still closed, face toward Canaan's hand.

"Keep them closed," Canaan said and Tork jogged back into the room when silently summoned. "Open your shirt," he told him and when it was done, he moved his palm to Tork's strong chest. Again, Vanny's face followed without use of his eyes.

"Nothing," Vanny said and Canaan dropped his hand. Tork stepped out and Bel instructed Vanny to open.

"You spent the past eighty-four nights investigating this electricity between us. To understand it. To learn something new."

"Eighty-four nights, yes," Canaan said with a new grin. "And to answer your unasked question, I enjoyed playing scientist with you." He looked up to Bel, who rolled his eyes. "I enjoyed the fuck out of every single moment."

Vanny's mouth curled into a grin and Bel wrapped a hand around the back of his neck.

"But when you walk through that door, I will not think of you again." Canaan meant it, but the nearly invisible smirk on Bel's lips told him his compatriot didn't believe his will was that strong.

"In a few decades, the Fathers will toss you together again and see where it is," the tall Elder said and wiggled Vanny back and forth. "Come. Our train leaves shortly. Kiss each other goodbye," he teased and dropped his hand.

"We're done." Canaan turned away.

With a soft sigh, Darcy Vandiver shuffled past his master and into the hall. When his footsteps descended the stairs, Bel pounded Canaan's shoulder hard.

"This schooling session took too long," he hissed, resurrecting his earlier indignation. "If I didn't have to catch this train, I'd pummel you senseless. Stuffing my lieutenant for three months isn't enough? He smells like shit with your blood—"

Canaan didn't allow him to finish. With a powerful shove, he pushed the gigantic Elder off his feet. Bel was up in a millisecond and the fight was on. Screw the train. They ran every evening. Canaan very well might be broken in half by the older and more experienced Elder, but they'd stay another night and he'd grab one more experiment with Darcy Vandiver. Good plan.

Brandon's Two Fixers

Darcy and Jersey Reconnect

Year 1949

"What's Master Brandon gonna do with *two* fixers?" The Lieutenant wasn't truly asking and Darcy only grinned, staring out the windshield. Then Sarna chuckled and said with his mouth to the side, "Jersey's never out of his sight as it is."

Darcy glanced his way and studied his profile. Sarna was big, not as tall as Darcy, but broader across the chest with a thicker overall set. He sported bushy brown hair, a three-day beard, and a stern hazel gaze. The Elder likely enjoyed his rugged look; based on what Darcy knew about Brandon, he chose companions based upon appearance first, talent second.

Sarna peeked right. He caught Darcy's eye only a millisecond before he cursed and faced front again. "Fuck me. *Shit!* Those eyes..." He comically pressed his crotch and shook his head. "You're worse than Jerz."

"He good?" Darcy asked, aware that Jersey enjoyed a sweet assignment handpicked by Elder Kilmeade.

"Oh, he's perfect." Sarna was still firmly pressing his lap. "Spends every waking breath either killing us with laughter at his crazy humor or giving us blue-balls with that crazy gaze."

Darcy smirked looking out the windshield. Jersey's ish-mikhan reputation was indeed the most famous, and Darcy did not disagree. No one got him harder than Kilmeade's first pup.

"I heard Master Brandon say you like to fight. That right?" Sarna asked and Darcy nodded.

By Darcy's seventh year, he stood taller than any proselyte in the lair's history. Before age twenty, he had grown as large as most of their Elders. This gave him the sturdiness to be trained in advanced sparring techniques, allowing the Fathers to assign him to the more pugilistic and physical leaders.

Sarna had asked, *you like to fight?* And he did. Darcy enjoyed all his work—be it battle, excellence with any hand-held weapon, as an expert in fitness and kinesiology, or as a release for an Elder's sexual energy. Darcy had never had a bad assignment and looked forward to each new sunset.

"You were with Elder Bel most recently?" Sarna asked and Darcy nodded, purposefully keeping his words few.

"Bel is huge," Sarna continued and took a deep breath, his eyes on the road. "He pummeled me a few times at Assembly. I remember hearing he had a fix-it man he could smash as well as fuck." Sarna chuckled once and sighed.

"You held your own?" Darcy asked without looking over, giving the man an opportunity to brag.

"Always," he said without pause. "How about you? How long did you last?" Sarna peeked right, but again, only took in Darcy's general shape. In his peripheral vision, Darcy watched him bite his bottom lip. "Did he knock you unconscious a lot?"

Darcy made a noise to interpret any way the lieutenant chose and ran his fingers through his hair, separating the strands. It had been a long night of travel and he anticipated a long hot shower with Brandon's Number One. His mind on Jersey and not on fighting, Darcy only partially attended Sarna's continued banter.

"Brandon doesn't knock us unconscious. *Hehe, shit,*" Sarna laughed and then rubbed his eyes with one palm. "Master Brandon used to spar with me all the time—I was his favorite for a decade—but he got bored. He's been through all the soldiers and will pummel any grunts passing by."

Sarna peeked then at Darcy's body and not his face. In Darcy's peripheral vision, the man's cheek twitched, his gaze locked to the area of Darcy's lap. He snapped his eye back to the road and shook his head once. "Are you the type that appreciates advice?"

"I am," Darcy replied and Sarna chuckled; the mere sound of his voice affected the soldier more than ever now that his state of arousal had nearly peaked. Darcy saw it often, especially among brethren who worked close to their Elder. These had less free time, which meant less time with whores, as well as less playtime with agreeable (and similarly stove-up) brethren.

"Then, here's what I suggest. Brandon isn't vicious, but he has phenomenal technical skill. My advice is twofold - don't hold back and learn his techniques sideways."

"I will."

Sarna nodded and mumbled in a deep voice, *"You will,"* before grinning and slowing the car to the speed limit. "Brandon doesn't fuck soldiers." He looked over and met Darcy's eye to blink in his direction. "I realize you're a high-ranking captain..."

His statement required a reaction, but Darcy didn't give him the satisfaction. Whether or not Brandon fucked him was irrelevant. Elders were fixed in a million ways, sexual release being only the most obvious.

Sarna continued, undaunted. "But I mean—look at you. Shit, he might make an exception. Judas Priest! I can't stop yammering." He laughed. "The word is that he won't use you for sex. He's going to allow you to fuck whomever you please."

He looked at Darcy again, who did not look back. Instead he watched out the windshield without a response.

"I heard a bit of news you should particularly enjoy."

His tone caused Darcy to glance left. The lieutenant was trying his best to get on Darcy's good side. Darcy met his eye and lifted an eyebrow.

Sarna took a deep inhale and licked his lips. "In thirty days, Elder Canaan will arrive to travel with us to Assembly. My captain said you two have history."

Darcy grinned and looked front. Stretching one long arm

across the distance between them, he squeezed Sarna's shoulder and left his hand in place. Yes, he and Canaan had history. His mind took the tiniest peek into their last meeting and blood rushed to his extremities more quickly than he expected. Sarna noticed.

"This stretch sure is deserted," the soldier said thoughtfully.

"Yes, it is," Darcy replied aware he'd lowered his voice. When he knew Sarna was looking, he leaned back and stretched out his legs. The Cadillac had plenty of room and he rubbed both thighs.

Beside him, Sarna added, "I'd like to spar with you right now."

Darcy flashed him a grin. "Pull in up there," he said gesturing with his right hand.

The black countryside rolled by with no moon, the stars obliterated by clouds and the hazy azure light caused by their special vision illuminated the landscape. An abandoned cow shed sat off the state road, its overgrown lane accessible through a broken gate.

"Sh-i-i-i-i-i-i-t," Sarna whispered and did as suggested. He crawled the Caddy to the structure, got out of sight of the road, and switched off the car.

"Get out," Darcy said opening his door.

Sarna did so and looked at him over the hood. "I must seem like the softest moron you've ever encountered," he said with a weak chortle. "Trust me when I say, I'm not. I'm Brandon's top lieutenant for a reason. I can't be bested—I've never been bested by a grunt."

"You want to spar or fuck?" Darcy asked teasing.

"Shit-shit-shit," Sarna said with comedy and grabbed his fly. "Jersey's the only fix-it man I've ever met and Brandon won't let me near him…"

Darcy grinned wider. The lieutenant hadn't been fixed. "Ahh, *ishy-szu*,"[13] he said and began his crossing to Sarna's side of the wide car. "I'll go slow."

Sarna may have had more to say, but he only left his lips parted

---

[13] One who's never been fixed by the Ish-mikhan (Rakum slang).

and watched Darcy come near. When close enough, Darcy cupped the man's bearded cheeks, feathering his fingers into the depth of the coarse hair and holding him tight.

"What do I do?" he rasped only inches away, his eyes on Darcy's mouth.

"Relax," Darcy sent telepathically, the man's thread throbbing in time with his racing heart.

"You're the expert," he sighed and softened his posture to receive Darcy's kiss.

"That I am," Darcy said as they touched lips, ready to show Brandon's top soldier what he did best.

Jersey recognized Darcy's heartsounds before hearing his familiar step. Then of course there was no mistaking his voice.

"Kazak, Lieutenant," Jersey heard him say at the foyer.

"Up there, last room on the right," Sarna replied and then his friend was on the stairs.

"Hold it together," Brandon teased rising from a gigantic pine desk in the corner. "You're coming out of your skin. Shit."

Jersey grinned and got to his feet. Brandon had hinted at a temporary lodger, but purposefully forced Jersey to guess who it might be. Now that he knew it would be Darcy Vandiver, his entire frame yearned to reunite with is favorite brother.

Darcy appeared in the open door. He looked directly at Brandon, offered a nod, and lowered his eyes with, "I am Darcy Vandiver. I will serve your will."

Jersey trained his eyes to his old friend and waited. Brandon made a few noises of approval before gesturing for the new guy to come close. When Darcy was within arm's length, Jersey grinned at him knowing he read him sideways.

"You are perfect," Brandon told him and placed a palm to Darcy's inner shoulder. Behind him, Sarna entered and stood near, but Darcy did not turn. Brandon remained in Darcy's gaze for a full minute without a word. When he spoke again, he withdrew his hand and motioned for Darcy to stand on his right, opposite Jersey on his left. He addressed Sarna facing them from the doorway.

"Darcy will spend the days with me, but other than that, I have no restrictions. Tell your soldiers."

Darcy remained expressionless, but Sarna sought his eye and manufactured a tiny grin.

Brandon turned his face to Darcy, looking up as he was inches taller. "I have some business in town. It is my will that you and Jersey reconnect while I'm gone. Before I return, shower well. Do not come to my bed smelling like these men—and do not shave. Keep your beard trimmed like this. Understand?"

"Your will is my will," Darcy said and Brandon nodded.

Then, without another word and without touching him other than the one time to the shoulder, the Elder left the room with Sarna close behind. When a few seconds elapsed, he looked to the right, his chin angled down to his friend a good three inches shorter.

"Look at you," Darcy told Jersey and took his face in both palms to kiss the corner of his mouth. "Almost big enough to ride the ferris wheel."

Jersey laughed. "I'm big enough to kick your freakish ass."

He held Darcy's forearms as the hands hadn't left his face. He had been clean shaven when they last met, but Brandon wanted every man in his pack to sport facial hair. He stared back into his pal's yellowy gaze and grinned when the blinking contest stretched into a full minute.

Finally, he squeezed Darcy's arms. "Making friends already,

I see," Jersey jibed noting his pal drenched in the lieutenant's aroma.

Darcy gave him a half-grin. "That's my new bodyguard," he said and dropped his hands to cross his arms. "We traded a few secrets."

"Always good to have a top soldier watching your back," Jersey noted, smiling at his remark. Darcy had no reaction but posed his next question in a soft tone.

"Elder Canaan's headed here next month?" He watched for Jersey to confirm. Darcy grinned. "I haven't seen him in years."

Jersey smiled back. "Elder Brandon is aware that the two of you might enjoy a catch-up."

"That is very true," Darcy agreed and looked about the room. "Looks like you have it made. This Elder is smitten. Sarna told me all about it."

Jersey chuckled and dropped into the nearest short couch. "They are all well-liked. Unlike most Elders, Brandon doesn't cause consternation for kicks." Jersey was thinking specifically of Canaan but remained mum.

Darcy saw through him and sat close. "That's what makes each Elder spectacular in his own right." He held one hand to his chest, palm flat and down. "Like your master prefers dwarfs, where Canaan enjoys more substantial meat."

"Hah!" Jersey barked with an unexpected chortle. "Don't start that; any Rakum alive will tell you Jersey is the very best ish-mikhan alive. Size is irrelevant."

Darcy laughed, his face to the ceiling. "Keep telling yourself that, little fella. Size doesn't matter. Size doesn't matter. Size doesn't..." Darcy's voice trickled off and he shook his head.

Jersey peeked at Darcy's surface thoughts and nodded with a grin. "Sarna told you correctly. Brandon doesn't need a gargantuan fix-it man's attentions. I have that covered. Let him pummel you senseless; that will be fun."

"I'm game," he replied easily and sighed. "Elder Canaan. I

wonder what he's been up to."

Jersey had no reply. Even though they both spent their lives with Elders, how the superior brains of their leaders worked remained a mystery. The only thing Jersey had learned for certain was that in no way did they process information like the rest of the population. They did what they wanted, when they wanted, and could do no wrong. To top it off, if they did something that could be perceived incorrect, no one would call them on it—it becomes right if an Elder does it. Every grunt learns the infallibility of their leaders in group lair and this faith delivered great comfort.

"I prefer to pretend he thinks about me," Darcy said following his stream.

"The Elders see that as a weakness," Jersey said in all seriousness.

"So be it," his friend replied quietly, looking forward, his arms resting on his knees. Darcy swiveled his face, his body slumped over his thighs. "If I ruled the world, you and me and Canaan would be together every sun-up. I'd never get tired of that. He rides me, I ride you, and round and round we go."

Jersey laughed and shook his head. "You have always been such a romantic." He softened his eye. "Let me tell you what Kilmeade told me about Darcy Vandiver. What you call your ish-mikhan leanings are a peek at your latent human nature. The seed of your breeder makes you infinitely fuckable and works just as hard to make you soft."

To his surprise, a slow smile approached Darcy's mouth as he listened to what their greatest Elder shared about his nature. "I am one of a kind," he whispered and sat up to put his palm to Jersey's thigh.

Jersey covered Darcy's hand with his own. "Let's recap and close out the Elder topic: Canaan's an asshole. Brandon is wonderful."

Darcy laughed a relieved sound and moved his hand up to the back of Jersey's neck. "I'll be sure to tell him you said that." With a gentle tug, he maneuvered Jersey close until he pressed his face into his hair. "Well, Elder's pet," he said then, his voice muffled, "what did your master mean when he said we should get reacquainted?"

"Oh," Jersey whispered and his left hand squeezed Darcy's near leg. "This was it. We're all caught up. Let's go see what they're fixing for dinner." Grinning, Jersey attempted to sit up and away.

Darcy did not permit him to move more than an inch, the grip firm at his neck.

"I'm serious," Jersey said even softer as Darcy opened his mouth wide against Jersey's throat and bit down with no real pressure. He made a few growling noises and brought his opposite hand up to cement their connection.

"Liar," Darcy whispered and suddenly made an about-face to climb onto Jersey's lap, straddling him on the soft cushion.

Jersey pressed both hands into Darcy's chest, laughing. "Get off, you gigantic baby!"

"Stop resisting!" Darcy snapped in between chuckles. Repeatedly, he attempted to kiss Jersey's cheeks as he whipped his face side-to-side. "JERSEY!" Darcy shouted and grabbed his chin in one hand.

"DARCY!" Jersey imitated at the same volume and shoved his friend from his lap with all his might. Darcy landed on his back and lay still, laughing with his hands resting on his middle.

"You're killing me," he laugh-talked. "If you don't fuck me soon, I'm dead…"

Jersey stood and looked down on him. "Who's the best?"

"Jersey!" Darcy brought up one palm to cover his eyes. "Emil Jersey is the best."

"Damn straight. Go to the bed," he barked at volume and yanked Darcy to his feet.

"Here we go," a voice from the hallway filtered in. Brandon's soldiers had returned from some errand, and although both Jersey and Darcy heard them come into the house, they didn't realize they'd interrupt.

"Close the door," Jersey said to him without looking over, his eyes in Darcy's, who sat on his knees in the middle of the thick comforter. The door closed quietly with the two soldiers in the room. Jersey grinned, face toward Darcy.

"I love an audience." Darcy unbuttoned his shirt, also not looking at their guests.

"If they pay attention, they might learn something," Jersey replied and only looked at the door when Darcy reached for his belt. "You idiots stay over there." Brandon wouldn't want their scent on his bedlinens.

The Rakum leaned against the door, eyes wide with anticipation. A rare treat—two *ish mikhan* plying their trades together. They'd have a great story for their pals.

Jersey tuned the man out and shoved his huge pal onto his back.

Canaan's Tag-A-Long
...Is Jersey's Little Project

Thirty days passed and Brandon did not call Darcy for sex, nor did he want him present when serviced by Jersey. He did, however, summon the giant fix-it man to the ring for nightly fighting over the rough rock floor of the raw cellar. Tonight, Canaan would arrive, and Jersey saw their master and his top soldiers out the door on their own business, leaving the ish-mikhan to welcome the visiting VIP. Currently, the house sat quiet, Jersey and Darcy waiting in comfortable silence, both reading from the Elder's extensive library.

Downstairs, the front door opened the sound of approaching footsteps reached their ears. In the opposite chair, Darcy rose to his feet and ran both hands through his long hair. He shot the name "Canaan" to Jersey's mind as the Elder's memorized scent traveled to their position.

The Elder said, *"Stand there till someone moves you,"* as he climbed the steps and Jersey tucked in his long-sleeved shirt. *"This is the shittiest welcome-wagon I've ever seen."*

Darcy bit his lower lip, his eyes saying they should have waited downstairs. Too late; within seconds, the Elder's hulky frame filled the open doorway. He met Jersey's eye a millisecond and then focused his attention to the tall figure on his right.

"Vanny, *Judas Priest!*" he said both fists to his hips. "Come close, you shit!"

Darcy crossed without hesitation and Jersey unlocked his feet to fetch luggage. He strolled past as the Elder grasped Darcy by the throat with both hands and yanked him into his space. When Jersey left the room, the Elder had pressed his face to the crown of

97

Darcy's head, mumbling words meant for his favored one alone. Jersey grinned and trotted down the steps.

A slender young man, mortal and not a Cow, stood in the foyer, his expression pensive. He held two carry-ons and swallowed hard when Jersey met his eye.

"Hey. I'm Jersey," he said to the kid with a smile. "What's your name?"

"Craig, Master," he said in a whisper.

"How old are you?"

"I'm seventeen, Master." His eyes darted about and he did not hold Jersey's gaze.

Jersey's head tilted to the side as he worked to figure the boy out. His scrutiny caused Craig's pulse to race so he smiled again and reached for one of the bags. "Let me show you where these go."

"Thank you," he said in the same soft voice, not meeting Jersey's eye for more than a moment each instance.

On the stairs, Jersey said over his shoulder to the boy, "you sure are timid. You need me to bust you up a little? Do they push you around?" Jersey was joking, but the boy answered as if he were serious, his pulse spiking even more.

"No, no way. They are nice. All of them."

Jersey peeked at his flushed face and chuckled, leading him the rest of the way in silence.

When they reached the large suite Jersey knew Brandon would want assigned, he gestured to the boy to set his parcel on the chaise. When the kid did so, Jersey set his beside it and stepped close enough to the boy to touch him. Craig didn't move away, but he inhaled sharply and held his breath.

"What's your story?" he asked without checking with Canaan, aware that he might get in trouble. Being the mischievous sort, Jersey didn't mind the thought of being punished. When the youngster hemmed, he asked again, more directly. "I can see you're not a Cow and you don't smell like sex, so what do you do for the Elder?"

The boy's mouth dropped open and he stuttered, "No! I... I... I carry stuff."

Jersey grinned and rolled his hand for more. "And?"

Craig's gaze skirted the room and he crossed his arms at his chest. "Master Canaan is my master. I do whatever he says."

Jersey sighed, unsatisfied with his answers. He turned his face toward Brandon's suite two doors down where Darcy could be heard tending Elder Canaan. At a normal volume, Jersey asked, "Master Canaan, can I drink your valet?"

As he spoke, Craig gasped. From the other room, the Elder chuckled and consented. Jersey looked back to Craig and winked, reaching for the boy's shoulder. Craig didn't resist but grew increasingly fearful.

"Don't eye my soldiers, asshole. They aren't fucking you this go-round."

"I've fucked Tork. He's pretty good..."

"Shut-it. So... you turn 239 this Assembly. I must be your present..."

"Maybe I'm your present. Did you think of that?"

"Still too full of yourself... I like this beard. Show me the rest..."

Jersey overheard Canaan and Darcy's conversation since they did not hide it. He knew Darcy favored Canaan above all Elders and because of that, the Fathers kept them apart. The difference between grunts and Elders was mostly in the mind—Canaan could go decades without even thinking about a favored brother, but a grunt enamored with an Elder didn't have that level of control.

As Jersey palmed his knife and gently reeled the frightened mortal into his embrace, he heard Darcy exercising his talents wooing and knocking his favorite Elder off his feet *literally*— Canaan enjoyed violence and by the time Jersey pushed his small knife-tip into Craig's inner arm, a loud crash of furniture sounded from upstairs.

"Holy fuck! Who's been instructing you?" Canaan barked as Darcy landed a double blow to his kidneys that caused him to grunt with surprise.

Darcy grinned at the rhetorical question and hopped out of reach. Elder Brandon spent his sexual energy on prostitutes, and if they were unavailable, he would turn to Jersey for release. He'd never been to bed with Darcy and used him strictly for physical exercise. He did not have to go into teacher mode for Darcy's keen mind to pick up every unknown bit of fighting skill used against him.

"If you use another Elder-specific technique on me, I'll—" Canaan began and Darcy slammed into him with his rounded outer shoulder, a balled fist simultaneously clocking the back of his sparring partner's head. He hadn't executed the move as smoothly as Brandon, but Canaan recognized it. Canaan's response was to spin around, come up behind Darcy faster than his eye could follow and lift him off the ground at the chest. Darcy was a couple inches taller than Canaan's 6'4", so his toes touched intermittently as the Elder decided what to do next.

"What'll you do, Master? What?" Darcy teased out of breath.

Canaan chuckled and lowered him to his feet without releasing so his front conformed snugly to Darcy's back. "I'll use it on Brandon properly and tell him this is from Darcy Vandiver."

The Elder had spoken close to Darcy's ear softly, romantically—the current wrestle coming to a close. His master remained there, his breathing already normal, heartrate only elevated because of the energy between them. In another long second of silence, Canaan moved his cheek a fraction against Darcy's jaw, still from behind and over his shoulder.

"Vanny, holy fuck," he said under his breath, stroking his smoothly shaved cheek to Darcy's trimmed beard. "From this point forward, you better have this beard when I see you."

"Your will is my will," Darcy responded and Canaan exhaled,

the arms about his chest loosening but in place. The Elder's arousal grew and he did not hide it. The aroma of Jersey's bloodmeal hit the air and Darcy concentrated on it with his eyes at half-mast. Canaan released him and Darcy swiveled to see him. He raised his eyebrows, leaving it to the Elder to share regarding his companion.

"The son of a Cow murdered in the night." Canaan spoke in a volume that alerted Darcy he was explaining to Jersey at the same time. "Barna arrived for his scheduled meeting, found the Cow's head blown off and a near-fatal wound in his kid's chest." Canaan lifted his fingers to stroke Darcy's facial hair. "I haven't found a use for him yet, but he amuses me."

Darcy grinned and enjoyed the way the Elder's eyes softened. All Elders liked Darcy, but Canaan favored him most.

"Narcissistic asshole," the Elder whispered. "What'd I miss?" he asked still close. "You were with Bel."

"He took a mate," Darcy said low, his eyes landing on the Elder's mouth. "She thought about me too much..."

Canaan grinned and brought his second hand to Darcy's opposite cheek. "Musta come after you, too." Darcy licked his lips with the same tiny smile and Canaan fanned his hands into his hair on both sides. "When Bel tires of her, you'll go back."

Darcy had made the same prediction and his eyes agreed. At that moment, from the other room, Jersey asked in normal volume, *"What can I do to help you with this kid?"*

"Find out if he—" the Elder began and Darcy covered his lips, stepping in closer to look down on him, using his height advantage.

"Think it to him, lazy-ass. This is my time," Darcy whispered too low for Jersey to hear, knowing the irreverence of his words made him deserving of immediate chastisement. But the Elder did not grow angry. He grinned beneath Darcy's palm and responded telepathically, including Darcy in the transmission.

"See if he has the propensity to do what you do, but don't force it. If he doesn't, find his strengths so I can exploit them; he's gotta

be good for something besides carrying shit around." Canaan paused, his eyes deep in Darcy's. He closed his fist in Darcy's long hair and yanked his head back hard. *"Try to get that petrified look out of his face. If he doesn't stop that fearful shit, I'm gonna turn him over to some folks who enjoy it."*

Darcy grabbed Canaan's available forearm with both hands to steady his balance, as he was still being held straining backward. The Elder raised his captive arm and pressed a long thumbnail into the soft skin of Darcy's throat, directly below his trimmed beard. The blood of a Rakum tasted much like warm dish water, yet Canaan often pulled blood from Darcy before they moved on with their fun. Darcy braced himself in the Elder's arms, closed his eyes and waited.

"You feel okay?" Jersey asked the boy who nodded, his fearful expression in place. Jersey had taken his blood gently, but enough of it so he had to give the boy a little energy boost. He and the kid were standing near the guest bed, a large King, and Jersey inclined his head. "Have you ever had sex?" he asked and then clarified with a grin, "With someone other than yourself?"

Craig shook his head mouthing, "no."

"I could teach you how to service Elders sexually," he offered point-blank since Canaan was specific about not increasing the kid's trepidation.

"No, please," he begged in a whisper refusing to look at the bed.

"Okay, here's the thing," Jersey told him moving them both to a sitting area with two loveseats facing one another. He waited for Craig to sit and he sat across, on the edge, leaning forward. "The scared act has to go. Your master hates it. I'm going to find a way for you to not be afraid. Understand?"

Craig made no move but was listening.

"What do you like to do for fun?"

"I-I like baseball."

Jersey watched his face so he'd add more.

"Dad drove a taxi and sometimes he let me drive."

"You like to drive?"

"Yeah..." he said in a low voice, his pulse no longer hammering.

"And? Speak, kid—I don't have all night."

"Mr. Barna—Master Barna—has a Cadillac He let me drive it some..."

Jersey nodded. Before the father's death, the teen thought Canaan's captain was a friend to his dad. Craig's heartbeat was normal now and breathing relaxed. The terrified expression had also morphed into a more agreeable countenance.

"Follow me," Jersey said and marched from the room. He wouldn't need to say anything to Canaan since the Elder would have heard every word. He led Craig to Brandon's garage and flipped on the overheads. Brandon collected cars and five sat in a line in the industrial-look space. "Do any of these cars interest you?"

Craig tried to hide it, but his eyes shimmered with lust at the sight and he slowly passed the first car, his hand gingerly and lovingly caressing the glossy hood. He tiptoed past until he reached the shiny black Ford.

"This looks like the car my dad drove back when he dated my mom..."

Jersey nodded—it was Brandon's favorite, too. Maybe if they took it out for a spin, Jersey could learn something useful about Craig for Canaan and make Brandon angry at the same time. As he pondered what his Elder might do to him for his cheekiness, he opened the driver's door and ushered Craig behind the wheel. When Jersey was inside, he opened the garage door and pointed to the keys sitting in the ignition. "Show me your stuff."

Craig actually smiled—it was small, tight, and to the side, but for the first time, Jersey saw more than a terrified future dead guy.

When the boy piloted them out of the garage and down the long driveway of the estate, Jersey leaned back, kicked his legs out long and sighed for Craig to hear.

"Which way?" he asked and cautiously stopped at the security gate, looking left and right down the dark road.

"Go right and then take the first left," Jersey replied and closed his eyes. He listened to the roar of the engine and when the kid had made the turn onto the main drag of town, he told him to "let her rip." It was two in the morning and traffic nil. If they attracted the local police, Jersey felt certain he could work that out as it happened. In five minutes, Craig made a different noise and he opened his eyes. The boy was grinning now, laughing to himself and pushing the speed limit on a straight stretch of county road. It was time for instruction and Jersey crossed one ankle at the knee and waited for the boy to glance over and know he was being watched.

"Yes, Master?" he said, voice soft but eyes smiling.

"Elder Canaan doesn't like the fear in your face. He's never hurt you, you told me Barna and the other soldiers never hurt you either, so here's the thing..." Jersey waited for him to nod he understood. "When we get back and you face Canaan or any other Rakum, think about how you feel right now. You should fear your master, but in the way you feared your father—respectful. Not as if we're about to attack you."

Craig licked his lips and glanced him a nod. "Yes, sir."

"Always be respectful, speak only when spoken to, and submit if any of them ever put a hand on you." Craig's lips parted but he stopped before saying anything. Jersey took a stab at his unspoken query. "You've been with the Elder a month. If none of them have touched you except for blood, they're not going to." He waited to see understanding in Craig's eyes. "Canaan wants you to prosper—he likes you. This means nothing to you personally because Elders are capricious—but it means that if you can please him, he'll not end you." Jersey grinned to soften the sound of his words.

"I think I understand..."

"I'm going to tell Canaan that you're a great driver so you'll do that for him. You'll still carry stuff and give blood," Jersey said and was glad the boy did not flinch at the idea. "But you'll get to drive. It will take us a few days to get to Assembly. You'll be staying with me and my master during the days—you might be restrained because we don't know you—but I'll make sure you're comfortable."

Elder Brandon pinged him then—he was at the house greeting Canaan and did not reveal his opinion of Jersey's use of his favorite car.

"I want to see this boy," his master sent at the end and Jersey audibly instructed Craig to turn back for the estate.

For the kid, he cleared his throat. "Elder Brandon is back— you'll meet him right-off. He might touch you, and neither of us have any control over that. Listen close and I'll give you a few pointers to make it less stressful in case he does. You understand?" Craig swallowed hard and nodded, but the fearful look hadn't returned. "My master doesn't mix pain and pleasure like Canaan does, so if he wants to touch you, he will be gentle."

Jersey paused and concentrated on every movie he'd seen and book he read that might help him comprehend the youngster's mindset regarding uninvited sexual contact. Ish-mikhan never experienced negative emotions regarding any part of their training, so it took him a few moments to choose his next words. Then his master sent a sentiment indicating he wanted the boy to watch. Jersey raised his brows with humor and sighed for Craig to hear.

"When we arrive, I will service my master and you will watch."

Craig's chin wrinkled as he pondered the statement. "Watch?"

"That is what I said"

"Okay," Craig said in a soft voice turning into the drive.

"If you get nervous or frightened, just think about this fun ride."

"I will," Craig said and carefully parked the car where they'd found it.

Even as the garage door lowered and Jersey led the boy to the mudroom, Brandon growled at him in his mind. *"Don't think I didn't notice which car you chose for this little schooling session..."*

"Yes, Master," Jersey returned with a false-tremor. *"Please don't hurt me. Please..."*

Brandon did not respond and when he reached the landing, his master stood at the top of the stairs and met his eye. The only emotion reflecting back was lust directed particularly at him; Jersey realized he'd get no punishment.

Elder Canaan appeared then, exiting Brandon's room, and he clapped his back before jogging down to Jersey and Craig. His blue eyes sought the boy's face and Jersey didn't look back, hoping Craig did as he promised.

"Who's this handsome dork you brought from the garage?" Canaan said at volume and squeezed Craig's face with one hand. "Much improved. MUCH!" he bellowed.

Brandon turned away and entered his suite and Darcy exited as he entered adjusting his clothing. He trotted down to Jersey and shot a finger-gun to the kid.

"He's a very cute little dork," Darcy said and followed Canaan out the front door.

Craig watched him go. "Who's that?" he whispered with wonder at Darcy's appearance.

Jersey started up the steps. "Don't speak unless spoken to," Jersey said at the same volume. Craig nodded and they resumed upward. When he pushed open his master's door, Jersey bowed low before Brandon and dropped to a kneeling posture. In his peripheral vision, after a very short pause, Craig mimicked the move and clutched both hands in his lap.

School in session.

106

Smashing Stone

Elder Canaan's Pummel Dummy

1950

"Double-time-it, ass-wipe. If I have to go in for you one more time—Shit!"

The telepathic instruction brought a smirk to Michael's mouth and Jesse took notice. "Poor Julius," he said to his companion as they trotted down the main hallway toward the East Wing. "We're late."

"You, not me, I hope," Jesse said.

The man could fight, but he worried too much about his face. Michael only grinned and increased his pace. He expected to be put into the ring with any number of Elders at this most celebrated Assembly—the first held in their new facility, deep underground in Nevada. The surprise Julius slipped would be the appearance of Michael's least favorite sparring partner, Elder Canaan. On his right, Jesse said the Elder's name under his breath, proving that as always, his partner read his surface thoughts. Michael sent a test thought to screw with him: *"I'm going to suggest he warm up on you..."*

Jesse turned his face; they had arrived. At the wide mouth of the open-floored space, Michael ignored his friend's glance to meet the eyes of their pack. Their master was there, Jack Dawn, taller and thicker than any Rakum present. Elder Tomás on his right and Elder Port opposite, both burly specimens—larger than

107

Michael, but not by much. Then, there were the grunts, the twins Jack favored, Beryl and Meryl, both dripping sweat and bloody from healed wounds. Kite, Gage, Hoss and Destin rounded them out. Michael had wrestled every man there with varying success, and although he could never best an Elder, their leaders enjoyed his ability and stamina.

Not caring that the masters would see his thoughts, he sent to Jesse's mind, *"Maybe Elder Canaan isn't coming."*

Then the muscled blond master entered from the anteroom, immediately locking eyes with Michael from twenty yards away.

"He wants you to warm up on his little boyfriend," Tomás said in a laugh.

"You and your shit-telepathy, damn, Mike," Jesse sent over and removed his suit coat, always dressed for a big-money business meeting. He lamented often that Michael should practice his mystical gifts and master some measure of all.

Canaan switched his attention, his grin to the side. "Come here, sweetheart," the Elder said, pointing in Jesse's direction. When Jesse stood six feet away, they squared off, Jesse three inches shorter and fifty pounds light. The females loved the man's handsome face, athletic build, and suave style, but all the brethren wanted to do was see him bleeding and small on the stone floor. Jesse was attending all these thoughts as Michael pondered and he sent a silent "shut-it," just before Elder Canaan slammed into him with gusto.

As always, Canaan allowed the grunt to give it his all; let him swing with every ounce of strength. Three times, the Elder absorbed powerful blows from Jesse Cherrie. Michael circled to stand with Destin to watch the show.

"Now," Destin whispered, timing his word with the moment Elder Canaan grew weary of letting the inferior succeed.

And Destin guessed right—Canaan dodged Jesse's latest jab and chopped the back of his neck as his mass past the Elder's position. Jesse was out cold in that one blow. He hit the rough concrete floor and Canaan turned his eyes to Michael.

"Okay, lover, I'm warmed up," he cooed and gave Mike the come-here gesture. "Let's make a little wager," he said getting into a crouch Michael recognized. "If I win, you come serve me in my quarters for the rest of assembly."

Michael responded with a string of expletives in their language and the other Elders chuckled at his bravado.

Canaan didn't smile. "I'm serious," he said, holding Mike's eye.

Maybe for a tiny millisecond, Michael felt a smidge of doubt before he squashed it. He was a blood-son of the High Father—no Elder would expect him to go to his knees like a common grunt. His entire life up to now, they never even asked. This is how he knew Canaan was putting him on, making a show for the grunts present. Decided, Michael put on an expression that would make the others think he believed Canaan's threat and dove into the battle.

Seven minutes later, he opened his eyes and focused on the unfinished rock ceiling of the underground space. It was five seconds before he recalled the pummel party and he angled his head to view the other occupants. The place had emptied except for Jesse, who leaned against the wall near the door, and he recognized Elder Canaan's back. Someone had indeed been requested to fix the Elder's woes and Michael struggled to a sitting position as the Elder shooed off the grunt and refastened his pants. He swiveled to see Mike, his shit-eating grin in place.

"Fuck, I'm spent," he said and swaggered to where Mike lay. "You were out so I had to take a raincheck." Canaan put out his hand and yanked Mike up with too much power. He caught himself a yard away and didn't hit the ground. "I made Jesse fuck you in your sleep, though. Do you feel weird? Your pants are undone, didn't you notice?"

Michael's eyes jerked down, his hands going to his belt—everything was as it should be. Canaan exploded in a peal of laughter and clapped him hard on the back. Michael absorbed the power, bending over and forward under the torque of the blows, and the Elder sauntered out.

Forcing a cough to clear the blood and phlegm from his airwaves, Michael stood erect and looked to Jesse.

"It was good for me. Was it good for you?" he said holding back a grin. His nose had been broken, set, and healed, but dried blood stuck to his whiskers and lapel. He shrugged his expensive suit coat on and took a step toward the door.

"That was a hoot," he said in a low voice as he passed Jesse and they both entered the hall. "My ass feels fine. I guess you have a finesse I never knew."

"Everybody loves Jesse Cherrie," he said at the same tone and they both chuckled.

No one would ever get Michael in that position, but he'd see Canaan again. That master loved seeing him smashed, always had. Of all Elders, why did this one focus his energy on Jack Dawn's favorite lieutenant?

"Let him fuck you and he'll leave you alone," Jesse said maybe provoking another fight.

"Don't help," Mike said and rubbed his face with his palm. Blood, sweat, and snot coated the skin; he looked at it, looked at Jesse and before his brother could escape, he slathered it all over the back of Jesse's coat. Michael took off running. With obscenities flying from his lips, Jesse did his best to get his revenge.

A
Wholly
Delicious
Addendum

The First Edition of this rebuttal ended here,
but then our world turned upside down. This second
edition includes events occurring after Last Assembly,
and the worst day of all, November 11, 2017,
when we lost our birthright.
At least I found Darcy.
~ Jersey
Penned December 2019

Jersey Meets Win and Avi

Blood, Sex, & Violence

Year 2015

Year 2015, the Ten Fathers are gone, and the Elders dispersed to the wind. Without the protection of the High Father, it is difficult to get the blood Jersey so desperately desired. Tonight, and by chance, he spotted a Rakum strolling out of a convenience store. A careful tail led him to an affluent neighborhood where the brother disappeared into a home after forcing entry.

The aroma of his victim's blood caused Jersey's head to swim and he yearned to join in. Finding volunteer blood had become nigh impossible and stealing it drew too much attention. As a result, he didn't imbibe often, which left him cranky and uncomfortable. Jersey crept toward the elegant front windows, hiding from neighbors or passersby, but not his brother, who would have heard his heart sounds no matter how silent his approach.

"Come inside, brother," the Rakum whispered in their language and Jersey quickened his pace.

"Kazak," he returned pushing open the front door. Jersey had no difficulty seeing into the gloom and at the end of the long hallway stood the unfamiliar brother holding the victim to his chest.

"Better hurry," the brother said offering Jersey the dregs.

Jersey jogged up and assumed possession. He brought the victim's seeping wound to his mouth and pulled eagerly. When the flow thinned, he ceased with an exhale, anticipating the buzz that accompanied every live blood meal.

Standing close with only the dying man between them, the Rakum whispered in a Southern drawl, "Name's Winston."

Jersey wouldn't spoil the moment by speaking and his eyes fell to the guy's dusty cowboy boots. Winston wore faded Levi's and a rugged flannel shirt. *Nice costume,* Jersey almost commented, but wasn't ready to look up; as soon as their eyes met, the guy would see— The buzz arrived. Jersey moaned low as the effects of the live blood barreled across his frame, then he did not suppress a shudder of ecstasy at the final pulse.

"Judas Priest, that's sexy," his brother whispered. "I never buzzed like that." Winston's back was against the wall and Jersey lifted one hand to brace behind him, allowing the now-corpse to slip to the tile. "You gonna thank me properly?" Winston spoke this time at Jersey's ear, possibly intuiting what he hadn't yet seen with his eyes. He sniffed against Jersey's throat. "You smell good. Did you bathe in that cologne?" The Rakum stood closer than necessary and his breath fell on Jersey's cheek as the tingling filtered away.

Finally, Jersey pushed off the wall with an exhale, eyes on his brother's shirtfront. The man was strong, wide across the chest and built to fight. Jersey licked his lips prolonging the inevitable; when a Rakum recognized his special status, something interesting always followed.

"Speak up," Winston said this time in his soldier voice, waiting for Jersey to meet his eye. "We haven't seen another brother in months."

Allowing a knowing grin, Jersey raised his gaze. Winston was a bit taller with dark blond, almost brown hair shaved close, fierce brown eyes, and a strong jaw. As their gazes locked, a smirk hit the man's mouth recognizing Jersey's distinction as ish-mikhan.

"Fuck me," he said in awe. "And you're gorgeous as shit!"

Jersey ignored the remark and peeked into the adjoining rooms from where they stood. Winston's blood pressure headed up as he remained close, moistening his lips. Jersey didn't attend any of it. Pre-Last Assembly, he'd been always prepared to see a brother's eyes big with pleasure. Now? In a world gone to shit? Whatever this Rakum thought, Jersey wasn't performing freebies. He was, however, accustomed to how his magnetism affected others so he changed the topic without moving out of Winston's space. The dead man was prodded aside by Winston's boot before he separated his feet shoulder width apart, waiting for Jersey to return his focus.

"You know this guy?" Jersey asked, nudging the corpse with the side of his foot, aware of his brother's hyping respirations.

"Look at me." Winston put an open palm to Jersey's chest.

Jersey refused to comply and looked instead to the man's hand on his shirt. "Do. You. Know. This. Man?" he repeated slower than before.

Winston huffed once. "Negative." He watched his own fingers slide across Jersey's shirt. "Look at me, *polcz-v'.*"

Polcz-v'—favored one—the endearment only the ish-mikhan received. Winston's behavior revealed that he had been fixed in the past and at the realization, Jersey's engine revved of its own accord.

"Brother, go with it." Winston ran his hand to Jersey's shoulder.

"I would expect better discipline from a Rakum captain," Jersey said low and the brother grinned, likely assuming the fix-it man was starting the dance. He wasn't.

"Maybe I outrank you," the captain said, his voice seductive. "I was bred in 1817. Does that do anything for you?"

"Makes me want to offer you a pacifier," Jersey said with derision, ignoring his flirtations and hundred years the guy's senior.

"I'll gladly suck your pacifier." Winston's second hand joined the first and he tugged Jersey's collar. "How about you take off this shirt?"

Weary of Winston's deaf persistence, Jersey said, "Your Elder would be very disappointed in your behavior."

Winston chortled and turned his exploring fingers to open-palm caresses of Jersey's chest muscle. He was good with his hands, *really good*, but Jersey steeled his resolve and awaited a response.

"I'll tell you what, fix-it man, the Elders are gone." Winston raised Jersey's T-shirt to place warm palms to his skin. "But your sexy brother is right in your face."

The Elders are gone. Jersey swallowed hard and Winston pulled them together by running both hands to his lower back.

"I can be an Elder for a night, baby-doll. Wait till you see my bang-on impression of Master Fawn."

A familiar Rakum heartbeat approached then and Jersey had his out. Casually stepping free of Winston's embrace, he turned for the sound. It was a brother he knew and had enjoyed in years past.

The newcomer entered the hall and exclaimed when he met Jersey's gaze, "Judas Priest!" His brother came into full view, his shirtfront stained with blood. He glanced over Jersey's shoulder. "Win, do you know Jersey?"

"I want to know him, but he's awful shy," the man replied, resuming his come-ons, this time his hands encircling Jersey from behind. He pressed his face into the back of Jersey's head for a dramatic inhale as both hands sought purchase lower, pushing beneath Jersey's waistband to hover in place, warm palms awaiting a formal invitation. "He's very ungrateful. I bought him dinner and everything."

Jersey sucked his teeth in slow motion. The captain's touch was pleasant, practiced, and polite. But he was so damn relentless. Jersey focused on Avi who inched in, requesting a touch-greeting. Their world had gone crazy and a brother didn't always know how to behave.

Goddammit! Jersey screamed inside. *Screw all this tiptoeing around…*

Closing the tentative distance with Avi, Jersey cupped his brother's neck to bump foreheads. Winston's contact followed. Before Avi backed away (and to spite Mr. Hands) Jersey held him in place to kiss his mouth for several seconds. His brother exhaled with a wide grin when released, aware Jersey was mostly skewering Winston's pride. Rebuffed, the captain gave it a rest. With a husky chortle, he stepped clear of both men.

"No problem, Mr. Fix-it. You won't be able to resist me forever. Ask Avi; he played hard to get for exactly one night."

"Brother," Jersey replied, eyes still in Avi's, "your dick will rot off waiting for me to fall for that lounge-lizard shit."

Winston slithered his tongue and chortled. "Take your time, handsome. This lizard knows how to stay distracted."

"I saved you some next-door," Avi said as his pal circumvented them both, "and she has energy to spare."

Within fifteen minutes, Win had taken his part of the female victim and the three headed for the quiet night.

"Come home with me," Jersey asked Avi his eye to them both. "I have a place better than this and its just across town."

"We miss you, too," Avi said with a grin, referring to the very small number of ish-mikhan at the time of Last Assembly. "We'll move in tonight." He briefly cupped Jersey's cheek and offered a new nod. "Win and I will take care of you; we'll make it like the old days."

Jersey shook his head. "I'll take care of me, brother."

"I'll protect you both for a little head now and then," Winston sang in a playful Cowboy voice. He passed them to reach the truck ahead of them. Jersey and Avi took their time, avoiding the light of the streetlamps.

"Winston's been my favorite companion for fifty years," Avi volunteered. "Fun to fight, fun to fuck, bossy as shit. All you have to do is get used to his hands."

Jersey grinned and broke into a jog to beat Avi to the SUV. Once there, he piled in the back, Avi sitting up front with Winston.

"I'll figure you out, Jerz." Winston said once they were underway. "We'll exchange secrets. I have special skills, too."

Jersey looked out the window. No mere grunt could measure up to the ish-mikhan in what they did best, but it was good to have friends who tried.

Within a week, it felt as if Avi and Winston had been his companions for decades. The camaraderie between them was different than pre-Last Assembly, and as difficult as it was to quantify, Jersey felt the best word was a mortal one: friendship. Centuries alive with literally thousands of brethren, and Jersey could take or leave their company. Everything changed after the first night with Avi and Winston after so many months alone. Jersey liked that they had fallen into a joint schedule—eating, sleeping, whoring, and if they planned it properly, feeding together. Between the three of them, stealing blood and hiding the corpse had become extremely doable. Tonight, their seventh sundown together, they had successfully cornered a transient, drained his blood, and hidden his body at the bottom of a forgotten pond. Now, it wasn't yet 2 AM and they were back in Jersey's stolen mansion, full, happy, and more satisfied than they had been in years.

"Okay! Okay!" Avi said loudly, sloshing his whiskey as he dropped onto one of the three short sofas.

Jersey had pulled the couch assortment into the center of the greatroom facing inward and many of their evening games took place there. Tonight's fun had yet to be named but all three pounded Jack Daniels in an attempt to alter their stark sobriety. Becoming intoxicated was a physical impossibility because of their metabolism, but if they drank enough in a short time, they'd buzz. Jersey wasn't feeling anything, but Avi sounded halfway there.

"*Okay what*, idiot?" Winston snarked and slumped into a

couch.

"A-legyob![14] I'll go first!" he answered and kicked out both legs. The way they were situated, his heels bumped Winston's shoe and he repeated the move with a violent stomp. "My favorite fight!"

Winston grew still, eyebrows up, interested in the game. *A-legyob: the best memory of blood, sex, and violence,* the Rakum's favorite three past times, in any order, at any one time. *A-legyob* was played mainly at Assembly when grunts grew bored over long days underground with nothing else to do once mandatory meetings were done. To avoid getting into mischief, *a-legyob* had grown into a decent game.

Jersey pondered his choices as he listened to Avi share about the time a brother knocked him unconscious in a sparring match. He then moved onto his favorite sexual experience, eliciting a snicker from Jersey who had had more sex than the two of them put together. When Avi shared his favorite blood-draw, Winston rose and brought more whiskey. He gently booted Jersey's toe, handling him with care, almost as a mortal man might a woman, even though Jersey was certain he could conquer either of them in a fight.

"You go next, Jerz," he said, his eyes flirtatious. As a captain, Winston's interest leaned toward violence, but he still worked every angle to get Jersey to bed. So far, he hadn't been successful.

Jersey leaned over his knees sitting adjacent to them both. "My favorite blood came from a ten-year-old foundling in Tijuana."

"Girl or boy?" Avi asked sipping his drink.

"Girl."

"Ah! You split her open afterward!" Winston said, making himself laugh.

Jersey regarded him with a sigh—he didn't fuck prepubescents unless commanded to by a superior. His talent was

---

[14] "The Best" or "favorite," Rakum Hungarian

bringing pleasure, the end. "Focus, idiot. I took her blood. It was pure. It made me wonder about bloodlines and breeding among humans."

Winston chortled. "You think too much."

Jersey continued as if he hadn't commented. "My favorite violence occurred in group lair."

"No, it didn't. Impossible," Winston remarked, mostly because the Rakum were not even teenagers when they left the lair.

Jersey pressed his point with a nod of the head. "I had turned eight and my ish-mikhan status was known. My days were spent in the proctor's bed, but when he wasn't around, the older students decided I was made this way for their jollies. Eventually they jumped me and got me to the ground." Jersey grinned at the memory, as vivid as if it happened last night. "They didn't even get my shirt off—I was amazing, with natural ability, because I had only just begun training in battle—you know how we are at that age." Jersey waited while his friends nodded, both picturing what he described, and he immensely enjoyed the attention. "In the end, three of them were unconscious. Gash put me under guard after that."

"Shit, we gotta spar," Winston said then, sitting up to lean over his knees. "I never would have taken you for a fighter."

"I'm positive I could best the two of you—at the same time."

Winston stood and towered over him, his belt at Jersey's eye-level. "Come on, baby-doll, right now. Let's see."

"Shut it, Win. Let's hear his favorite sexual encounter." Avi slapped the air and their friend settled back down.

"Was it an Elder? You miss those shits more than you should," Win said looking Jersey in the face. "How many Elders did you fuck?"

"You can't fuck an Elder," Avi replied for him. "They fuck *you*."

"Is that right?" Winston asked Jersey. "Those Elders pitch? All of them?"

Jersey licked his lips. The Elders were gone or hiding from Rufus, so for the first time in his life, he could share their secrets. He decided he would. "In general, yes."

"In *general?* Who let you fuck him? Oh, shit, I gotta know!" Winston kicked at Avi who also nodded. "Kilmeade? It was Kilmeade, I know it. He was an arrogant shit. Fuck! I hated him." He swiveled his face to Avi. "Remember when I told you I lost three days?" Avi nodded and he turned back to Jersey. "Kilmeade zapped me unconscious and left me behind. If my brothers hadn't found me before sunup, I wouldn't be here today. Fuck him."

"How did you provoke him?" Jersey asked knowing Kilmeade hated soldiers.

Winston wiggled his eyebrows. "I took too long getting out of his way when he passed by." Jersey huffed and Win nodded. "So, which Elder did you ride? Kilmeade?"

Jersey's smile fell, it hadn't been Kilmeade, but he missed him the most of all. "No, my last Elder. Master Brandon."

"Brandon used to take it, eh?" Winston sucked his teeth. "I didn't know him very well."

"Me neither," Avi said. "He was handsome, though. I tried to get his favor once at Assembly, but his entourage was tight."

Jersey grinned. "He would've liked you."

Avi enjoyed the compliment and brightened. "Was he your favorite sex?" he asked returning to the game, but Winston grunted an interruption.

"Wait. With Brandon, how did you know? How you go from taking to giving when your partner can end you with a thought?"

Jersey shrugged one shoulder, only an ish-mikhan understood Elders in that way. He decided Winston, in particular, couldn't learn anything so metaphysical. Because of this, he structured his reply for his cognitive limitation.

"Elder Brandon was braver. I never thought he was the only one who wondered about it. Elders pride themselves on their 'I must always be learning' tenet but drew the line at fucking.

Kilmeade said it keeps them above."

"But Brandon had his own ideas," Avi said with a new smile.

Jersey agreed. "Brandon asked me to describe it and I knew from the first question where we'd end up."

"You knew because you're trained to know what Elders want," Avi said to himself.

"That and what we all know: Elders don't waste words. When he asked me about it, I knew he was in learning mode."

"So..." Winston said suddenly more animated. "What did he think? Yay or nay?"

Jersey didn't like the guy's intensity, as if this information lessened Brandon in some way. It should be the other way, that the Elder seemed greater, but they were grunts; how could they comprehend?

"Yay, very much yay," Jersey said and leaned back. Fucking an Elder had been a pinnacle and Jersey did not think anything for the rest of his life would come close to measuring up to that experience. He stiffened at the memory and tugged at his jeans. Win noticed and laughed to the side.

"You ready to hear my favorite sexual *a-legyob?*" Jersey asked.

"Yes, shut up, Win," Avi said and leaned forward. "Tell us."

Jersey waggled his eyebrows. "Do ya'll know a fix-it man named Darcy Vandiver?" Even saying Darcy's name caused physiological changes across Jersey's system and he let them flow. Maybe the whiskey was finally dulling his staunch carefulness. Both of his friends answered in the negative.

"Your favorite is another ish-mikhan?" Avi asked with wonder and Winston agreed.

"How in the world did ya'll stand it?"

Jersey grinned; his pal was right, it wasn't easy. Their magnetism worked on each other even more than the rest of the population.

"Wait. I call bullshit. Your best *a-legyob* can't be this Darcy guy." Winston watched Jersey for a reply. "Describe him."

Jersey smiled at the sudden photographic memory of his pal's face. "He's handsome—you'll never see a better-looking Rakum. And he's tall, a *mountain,* six-foot-six and hard as stone..."

"Taller than me?" Winston stood and put a hand on his head. "Here, stand up. Pretend I'm Darcy. Measure us. How much taller to I need to be?"

When Winston reached for Jersey's bicep, he gave the gentlest tug. Jersey liked his consideration and smiled again, rising to his feet. He stood toe-to-toe with Winston in the circle of three sofas. Winston didn't touch him, only patted his own head and asked again for Jersey to compare their heights.

"You need another three inches," Jersey said with a small grin.

Winston headed for the foyer. Jersey and Avi followed him to the foot of the stairs and Winston stepped on the first step before turning back to face his friends. He parted his feet.

"Compare this," he said in a softer tone, holding Jersey's eye and inviting him to come close once again with one palm open, up and extended. "Is this right?"

Jersey liked the game. He stepped into Winston's shadow and stood close, now his friend's chin was level with his forehead.

"This is closer." He pretended to consider Winston's upper body, measuring his ribcage by spreading apart his hands, still without touching him. "Darcy has incredible muscle tone, wide and developed across his chest."

As he finished his thought, Winston pulled his T-shirt over his head and dropped it to the hardwood floor. This brother's body was thick and wide, not tapered like Darcy's, but he emanated heat and Jersey's palm longed to make contact with Win's abdomen.

"Like this?" he asked very low, his eye in Jersey's.

Jersey's hand had been hovering in fake measure-mode and Winston tenderly maneuvered it to touch his skin.

"It's pretty close," Jersey said and allowed Winston to move his hands for him, across his musculature.

"What else?" Winston's voice had fallen nearly inaudible.

"Darcy's lips," Jersey began and stopped. He brought his fingers to his own lips and ran across them while holding Winston's eye. Winston lifted his hands and cupped Jersey's cheeks in warm palms. He leaned down to touch their mouths and the action was so very close to Darcy's. The height difference, the tenderness, and the excitement in the air. Their lips touched and in Jersey's mind, suddenly it *was* Darcy. Back from wherever he was. His favorite companion of 100,000 brethren. His best and most beloved partner in their trade. The one man he wished he had never let out of his sight when the Rabbit ruined their lives forever.

Winston closed the kiss, leaning out inches to see Jersey's expression. *"What else?"* he whispered again, pulling Jersey into him by the contact still on either side of his head, making sure the front of his jeans would press to Jersey's middle. *"I'll be Darcy Vandiver, baby-doll,"* he said in the same quiet tone, dropping another hot kiss to the corner of Jersey's mouth. *"You lead and I'll follow."*

Jersey decided the words were done. With a gentle inhale he ran his hands into Winston's short hair and pulled their faces together himself. Avi melted from his awareness as Winston kissed him like his old pal, walking them both to an adjacent room where a small futon worked for whatever an *ish-mikhan* and his imaginary lover might need. Winston finally got his way and Jersey didn't mind one bit; he had been a fast learner indeed.

Going Human

Try Not to Kill Your Brother

2017

Shirtless and relaxing alongside Avi on the couch, Jersey rubbed his belly in an absent manner, eyes on the television. Winston had pulled up a horror movie and for the moment, the nude teenagers on the cement floor hadn't noticed the monster bugs in the shadows. He and his brethren had fed well, locating a transient behind the burned-out paper mill, and now they sipped beers, full and comfortable, awaiting the sun. *Three hours until sunup,* Jersey counted inside, as every Rakum knew at a cellular level where the sun sat on its track.

Still rubbing his middle, enjoying the tickle of the hair to his palm, Jersey flicked his eye to Win. The brother sat in a recliner cattycorner to he and Avi on the sofa, his face to the TV. Onscreen, a mutant insect crawled into the breasty teen's hair as her boyfriend rammed into her with gusto. Jersey watched her nipples, his mind wandering to the last woman he fucked as his own hand fell still. The Cows were gone, but females still found him beautiful. If he fancied a pussycat, he knew where to find one. Presently, Avi's left palm assumed the task of rubbing Jersey's stomach in similar circles and Jersey grinned without turning. Avi preferred men and Win would fuck a cantaloupe—anything moist and warm inside suited his tastes. Once on a bet, he'd seen Win screw a horse. Jersey pivoted his eyes to Winston's profile. When

124

it came to sex the biggest difference between the three of them was only Jersey refused to force sex. He didn't mind if they raped the entire city, but why do something he didn't want to do? He had no master. Part of their shitty new existence meant each man was on his own.

"That's a good boy, goooooooood boy," Avi cooed, moving his gentle and rhythmic stroking toward Jersey's waistband. He allowed the fingers to intermittently break the barrier and come back out toward his sternum. Jersey gave him a wink and looked back to the screen.

Winston turned at their movement. "Watch the movie, shit!" he hissed and faced front again.

Avi instead rolled onto his left which made petting easier. He put more ardor into each pass and leaned close to bury his face in Jersey's neck. "Let's go to bed, baby doll," he whispered between soft kisses.

Jersey still faced the movie and a scream erupted as a horde of alien roaches covered the woman's tits and she disappeared. The young man with her was saved the embarrassment of showing his junk eaten up by bugs as the camera panned away, on to the next scene. Avi had worked his mass in front of Jersey's right shoulder so Jersey brought that arm to rest around his brother's upper back. Winston looked at them again and gained his feet. He stomped to the couch and looked upon Jersey, hands to his hips.

"You requested this idiotic movie," he drawled with a thumb to the television. "If you're gonna fuck anyone, it's gonna be me. It's my turn, Avi, and I will break you in two if you try to jump the line."

Avi did not lift his face from Jersey's jaw and said against his skin, "Chill out. I'm only getting him primed up for you."

Jersey grinned, it was a good game having his roommates focus their energy on him. He watched for Win's reaction. With a slow blink and a twitch in his cheek, Win turned away for the basement.

"I'm hitting the shower. And Jerz, you sure as fuck better be down there in seven minutes. Got it?" He left without a reply.

Jersey would go—it was their game. He loved being adored and even though they could all sleep together—and they had—sometimes it was nice to be singularly attended.

"I thought he'd never leave," Avi said in his throat, now slurping his tongue around Jersey's earlobe. They had lived together two years and his brethren had learned his buttons. Jersey's right palm sat quiet against Avi's shoulder blades and he rest his left flat to the cushion. Let Avi do all the work, it was his turn anyway.

The shower went on in the basement where they would sleep the day away from the sun. If he was headed down, he needed to go. Reading his surface thoughts, Avi rolled even more over his left and draped his right leg across Jersey's thighs.

"Let's piss him off," he said low in Jersey's ear. Without asking, his fingers unbuckled Jersey's belt and began with the button. "We can end this night in an all-out brawl."

"Sounds good," Jersey whispered, now closing his eyes and Avi went to work lower, perfection in his every suckle, squeeze, and lave. His brother made a sudden change in the play by hopping up to straddle Jersey and look him in the face.

"Let's make this work," he said in Jersey's eye, and with a mischievous grin he thrust his pelvis once. Jersey smiled too and his brother swooped in to lock their mouths.

Then the universe flipped upside down.

Jersey flushed from his forehead to his toes in a cascading wave of nausea, jerking backward into the sofa cushion, his actions unintentionally knocking Avi to the floor. The room grew darker and the television brighter as a heavy stone grew where Jersey normally felt his stomach. It was fifteen long seconds before he gathered his wits enough to look at his brother on the floor. Avi's eyes were enormous.

"What the shit?" Avi hissed. Shaking hands palpated his own

chest, his face, and then he propped onto his knees to shove a hand down his pants and examine his genitals. "What's wrong with me? Say something. I think I'm going deaf!" Avi inhaled, his fear evident.

Fear? SHIT!

Jersey shook his head in a tiny movement and pressed his palms to his body in a similar manner. The answer to Avi's question whispered across his subconscious and he screamed inside, *No way. No way. No way. No...fucking...way...* When their third brother shouted, "WHAT THE FUCK!" in the basement, Jersey stood tucking his ruined erection into his jeans and re-securing his belt. When he turned for the hall, he halted after one step. His body felt heavy, as if he'd donned a suit of armor. He forced another step, and then another, and behind him Avi followed posing his questions to the air.

"Shut up, Avi! Just SHUT UP!" Jersey belted aware that he had not yelled at either brother in anger since they met.

Anger? SHIT!

Stark naked and dripping water, Winston approached as they reached the basement floor. He met Avi's and then Jersey's eye, shaking his head side to side.

"No way," their brother said and reached Jersey to put a hand to his chest. Win cupped, squeezed, and prodded the muscle of Jersey's upper body and then his own, still mouthing, "no way."

"What? What is it?" Avi said in a high-pitched voice. "What's happening?"

Jersey put his hands to Winston's body and in a similar manner, rotated around to examine the broad surfaces of his muscled back.

"What? Judas Priest!" Avi said, near panic.

Panic? SHIT!

Fear, anger, panic – his inner mind listed off emotions, emotions Rakum did not possess.

"We're mortal," Jersey said in a very small voice his eye

coming to rest in Winston's. "Fucking mortal."

"Mortal," Winston said just as low, holding Jersey's gaze with ferocity. Avi began to screech, exclaiming there must be another explanation, but Jersey and Win had no doubt.

"What do we do? What do we do? Who did this? WHAT THE SHIT IS GOING ON?" Avi's queries crescendoed and Winston clocked his jaw with a vicious right hook.

"Shut your hole, Avi, or I'll smash your face in!" he barked standing over his brother.

Avi had landed on his back and he remained there, eyes trained to the dark ceiling where a single bulb threw 40 watts of light across the basement. Blood ran from the side of his mouth—it wasn't red, but it also wasn't Rakum-black.

Winston lifted his fist, rotated it to see his knuckles. The skin split over the first and second joint, seeping a similar half-n-half fluid from the wound. Jersey stepped into him and taking the hand in his fingers, lifted the blood to his lips. He tasted it and when it had rolled around his palate a few seconds, Win tasted it too.

"What?" Avi said in a whisper, his fingers smudging the trickle on his face and then bringing the sample to his tongue.

Jersey's bloodlust had disappeared; he knew it down to his deepest parts. The metallic flavor of his brother's blood should have at least tickled his hunger, but nothing happened. From his housemates' expressions, they sensed the same thing.

"Winston," Avi said then, using a voice they had only heard in mortals. A sound of terror and impending death.

Win looked to Jersey. "You're the master," he whispered, piling the responsibility upon the oldest among them. "Now what?"

Jersey held his eye three long seconds, his mind as clear as ever, his memory as sharp, his intellect intact. They all knew of brethren who had turned mortal on purpose, accepting the yoke the Rabbit Beth Rider offered them at Last Assembly, but it had been voluntary. Why had the three of them turned human at such a random moment?

Jersey blinked and put a comforting palm to Win's shoulder. The sun was upon them, the house upstairs locked down. For the next eight hours, he and his two brothers would hash it out, phone Rakum they knew, get to the bottom of the issue. Jersey put out a hand to Avi and jerked him to his feet. By sundown, they'd have an answer, and if Avi could keep his cool, they wouldn't have to kill him before then. First order of business? Jersey brought both men close with his arms across their shoulders. It was mortal. It was a hug. But somehow, it gave them courage to face what lay ahead.

That previous chapter haunts me still. Now you will read how we handle being human. Amazingly, we're still better than humans in every department.

~ Jersey

2020

Where

are they now?

In this final section, read about:

- ➤ Jersey (the adorable)
- ➤ Darcy (the perfection)
- ➤ Winston (the sex addict)
- ➤ Avi (the pining)
- ➤ Simon Miller (sexy Cow-man)
- ➤ Hester (the other ish-mikhan)

The Last Battle, *as we're calling it, took place in Winter 2018, and is covered in the novel* **Conundrum.** *This scene has sex in it and was not included. I think it's important.* ~ Jersey

Motherfucking Darcy Vandiver

Winston and Darcy

Year 2018

THE SET-UP (without leaking plot elements): *When Jersey goes to speak to Roman in private, he leaves Darcy, Win, and Avi behind at the hotel. This is what the guys were up to while Jersey was away.*

"Want anything from the lobby?" Avi asked, already opening the door to exit.

Winston said no and his companion of the past fifty years disappeared into the massive luxury hotel. Taking a deep breath and reclining on the neatly made bed, Winston covered his eyes with folded arm, his mind racing with too many threads to process. Then, the shower went on next door and he turned his head.

"Motherfucking Darcy Vandiver," he whispered in the quiet room, sorry the man returned to mind. He'd first laid eyes on him three days earlier, the image forever burned into his retinas. It wasn't like when he met Jersey; they had been fully Rakum then, hunting the mortals and partying as if there was no tomorrow. Sure, he'd needed to bed Jersey as quickly as possible, but this fucking Darcy... They were mortal now. Why did he affect Winston so dramatically?

Winston cursed under his breath and sat up. At the same time, the pipes between their adjoining rooms told him the most beautiful man he had ever seen was leaving the shower stall, nude

131

and wet.

"FUCK!" Winston said aloud and stood. He turned a small circle before heading for the hall. The door between their rooms was bolted on Jersey's side—he'd already tested it—so he stepped into the hall and knocked on Darcy's door, two hard raps, soldier-style. Darcy had also been a captain, which only intrigued Winston all the more. How many soldiers did he fix in his years? Thousands. And Winston never even heard of him until he met Jersey in 2015.

"It's Winston," he called close to the jamb. *Shit, whatever it takes, just come to the goddamn door.* "Can I talk to you—"

The door popped open as if the knob had been turned and released. Winston touched the wood and the doorway widened enough to see Darcy walking away, a bath sheet around his trim waist, his hair toweled but still damp. Winston completed his entry, closing the door and hearing the automatic latch. Still facing the opposite direction, Darcy held up one finger, busy with his phone, leaving Winston staring at his impossibly wide back and muscled shoulders. Winston formulated what he wanted to say while he waited and then Darcy chuckled to himself and turned.

Shit, even his turn was much too graceful for a mortal man. Winston covered his crazed thoughts with a tip of his chin. "Whatcha got?"

Darcy grinned wide, biting his bottom lip and then scraping it with his teeth as he approached. "Jibing Jersey," he said, his crazy deep voice bouncing off the walls. Winston chuckled like an imbecile unable to think of a better response.

"All Jersey does is eat and fuck," he said bringing his gaze to meet Winston's. Winston huffed, his mind racing with how to resist his body's clamor and after a moment, Darcy looked back at his phone.

Shit! Winston said inside. When the guy turned, he had felt physically released. It wasn't fair, it wasn't natural, and it wasn't mortal. How could a former Rakum fix-it man still hold such power? Darcy stepped for the over-sized lavatory, dropping his towel in the doorway and disappearing around the wall. None of the brethren were shy, but surely Vandiver realized how he tortured his guest. *Surely.* Winston blinked and concentrated on the design in the carpet. Ten long seconds passed and he wasn't winning the war of his mind, his thoughts refusing to be corralled.

As a Rakum, they possessed superior compartmentalizing skills. Each brother knew how to focus down and drown out the world. But they were mortal now and Winston could only think about touching the ripped abdomen of the man in the next room.

"Miről akarsz beszélni?" (What did you want to talk about?) Darcy asked in their language still out of sight. *"Varish Avi?"* (Where's Avi?)

There's my answer, Winston thought and licked his lips. Why else would Darcy use the old language if not purposefully driving his brother insane? Winston cleared his throat and swallowed. In a stern voice, he replied, "He's downstairs. I have to say something to you, Darss. It's important."

Darcy poked out his head, shirtless and now wearing dark blue boxer-briefs. "What's going on?"

When Winston didn't immediately reply, the brother returned to the main room and approached, stopping twenty feet away. He waited for Winston to speak, both hands finger-combing his cinnamon-brown hair behind his ears. Winston's eyes fell to the man's chest where soft brown hair stretched across his pecs. A small noise escaped and Darcy wrinkled his brow.

"What's up?"

"I need to apologize for my behavior. From when you picked us up until our adjustment meeting." Winston looked back into his face. A few hours ago, the tall Adonis felled him with one blow, commanding that he never touch Jersey again. "I've been a total ass and I don't want that between us. I think it's a mortal thing—I don't want hard feelings." Winston paused waiting for Darcy's reaction. His face remained open and listening, and he hadn't agreed or disagreed. Winston added, "I've been seeing a therapist. I texted her after our fight and she said I need to apologize."

Again, Winston waited for a reaction. A Rakum would never utter any of what he just said, but the Rakum were gone and in their earlier argument, Darcy had preached about moving on to the *New Way.*

"Apology accepted," Darcy responded without expression. "Therapist, eh?" he said and then added, "I saw one too, in January, after it happened. He'd been a Cow to Desi out of Miami."

Winston sighed. "Mine's a woman, but she knows about the Rakum. She's helped me a lot."

Something about his humble sentiments caused Darcy's expression to morph. He stepped closer, still out of reach, but he smiled, his dimples hurting Winston to see.

"What's going on tonight?" Darcy asked and after a tiny hesitation, he stepped close enough that if either of them lifted an arm, they'd touch. Winston shoved his hands in his pockets.

"I wanted to ask you about the Maker. What about this God shit?" Winston pulled his shoulders to his ears. "I mean, it's true, right? So... do we have to become believers? What happens?" Winston cursed under his breath, hating the sound of his own voice. But Darcy returned his gaze with soft eyes and an understanding tip of the chin.

"It must be true," he agreed in a quiet tone. "Kilmeade, Canaan, Roman, Yosef," he said, rattling off the names of Elders known to believe in the God of the mortals. Canaan was still intact, but he believed. "Father Damien and Father Theophilus," Darcy continued, still speaking in an almost whisper.

Winston nodded absently, but now he felt the man's breath fall on his skin, smelling of peppermint, and Darcy's aftershave, masculine and heady. As if from another world, he saw Darcy reaching for a pair of slacks he'd draped on the end of the bed where they stood. Winston covered his hand and met his eye.

"Please don't."

"Don't put on my pants?" Darcy asked with a half-smile and he stood, leaving the clothing where it lay. "What else did you want to see me for?"

Winston hemmed. He didn't want anything from Darcy and he wanted everything. He parted his lips to reply, but nothing intelligible happened.

Darcy watched him a few more seconds and then broke into a sincere grin. Holding his eye, Darcy reached for Winston's wrist and manually placed the hand over his heart. Winston didn't look, but the man's chest hair tickled his palm and brought a grin. When Darcy gave him the tiniest wink, Winston ran his fingers across the muscle, his body coming apart in a rush.

Then in a quick movement, Darcy stepped in, reducing the distance between them to nothing. Now the man's bare chest touched Winston's shirt, and because Winston stood shorter, he looked up to see Darcy's grin going to the side.

"You want to fuck the fix-it man?" he asked, his voice rolling across Winston's psyche. He cupped Winston's face with both hands. "I don't mind. Unlike my little Jersey, I've accepted this mortal skin. I know who I am." Darcy leaned in enough to brush his lips to Winston's cheek, first the left and then the right.

Winston couldn't breathe, his arousal so great. He understood the ish-mikhan were trained exclusively in sexual matters, that there would be no greater lover for anyone than a Rakum fix-it man, but to have this one giving it away? It was surreal. As Darcy continued to ply his skills, nimble fingers deftly unbuttoning Winston's shirt, he mumbled his question through a parched throat. "Why?"

Darcy paused his attentions to lean out and catch his eye. His grin returned and he pecked Winston on the lips, once, twice, and then longer. "Because you need it, I have it, and why not?"

His reasoning was amazingly Rakum-like, but Winston didn't allow his mind to ponder it any further. He finished removing his shirt and worked his belt. The Rakum were gone, but he remained, and the most beautiful man in the world was helping him undress. He'd figure out the spiritual stuff tomorrow; tonight, he'd clear his head with Darcy Vandiver.

Wooing the Cow-Man
Avi & Simon

Year 2020

"How'd you convince him to come all the way up here? Was the team in town?" Winston asked without diverting his attention from the television.

Avi didn't reply but passed through the den to the stairs. By the time he reached his room, he heard Win rise from the couch with a noisy grumble and tromp up the steps.

"Stop the whiny-baby-shit; you know I hate that," his friend groused, fists to his hips and blocking the exit with his body. "I'm listening. Tell me what he said."

Avi pulled on his socks considering his long-time roommate's sincerity. Winston didn't suffer loneliness or despair. He'd found a group of mortals that shared his affinity for drag racing; the adrenaline and common-leanings fulfilled him when they gathered for their two- and sometimes three-day meets. Also, Winston wasn't lonely for physical attention—he had girlfriends (plural) among them and occasionally, when drunk (or the group was on hiatus), he'd sleep with Avi, just like the old days. But with no outside interests so far, Avi only had Winston.

"Avi," Winston pressed, stepping close and dropping his tough-guy stance, "what about Jerz? He get serious about that woman? Did he finally drop out?"

Like an emotional vampire, he absorbed his pal's closeness a moment before answering. When Winston was near, it was easy to sink into despair about how the world had changed. His pal knew what he was doing and he grabbed his neck to squeeze and release. He then walked back to the door and asked again.

"Jersey get married?"

Avi sighed. "Last month, and he got Jesus." Avi shook his head, unable to comprehend it; Jersey had been their people's most famous fix-it man, he could, for the rest of his (mortal) life, write his own ticket with any surviving brother, and any human, for that matter. But he chose the mundane walk of a common husband and father, still best buds with his former *ish-mikhan* mountain of man-meat, Darcy Vandiver, who chose the same way: God, Family, Country. *Disgusting.*

"Vandiver, too, I guess," Win said and didn't need Avi to nod. His cheek tucked in with a tsk. "I asked him to come up here."

Avi whipped his head around. "And?"

Winston shrugged. "Who knows. You have no idea what you're missing. I mean, shit."

Avi tucked in his dress shirt with an agreeing hmph. He hadn't had the chance. Winston somehow grabbed time with the man the week they met him, but it all went down while Avi was out to the store. *Buncha bullshit.*

"If he shows up here," his friend said and whistled, poking at Avi, "you better grab some sack time. He won't be available forever."

"He's joining up?" So many of their brethren had chosen to follow the mortal God. Avi believed He was up there but didn't want to know more.

"Fuck, I don't know if he'll go through with it. He's too much deliciousness for that." Win clapped his hands. "Okay, so Simon flew in to see you? Just you, or me, too?" Winston added the last part for fun, his grin showing as much. "Is he still straight? You know he is—humans don't just *go gay* because a sexy Rakum chases them." Winston watched Avi closely, maybe really wondering if he had things confused. Simon had been a Cow to Javier D'Millier before the shit of Last Assembly and when Avi met him, something clicked, even if it was one way and only in his pants.

"Fuck you. I understand mortals," he said and began forward.

Winston blocked his way and grabbed his bicep. "You want to be wittle friendie-friends with the Cow-man? He let you jerk him off because he was shit-faced; that wasn't a date. You remember the lecture he gave you after?" Winston paused, still holding Avi's eye like a lair proctor. "I'm not letting you by until I'm convinced you're not doing all this to get him to sleep with you."

Avi crossed his arms and stared his friend down. He didn't *plan* to seduce Simon Miller, but the man was extremely attractive and they intended to have dinner and drinks… The clock clicked to seven and Avi had run out of patience.

"Move aside, Winston," he said without humor. "I don't want to force you aside." They hadn't sparred in almost a year, but before the world went to shit, they had kept in top form with constant two-man wars. Winston's grin returned, a new fire in his eye. He wanted to fight, he missed it. Avi truly only wanted to leave and pick up Simon at his hotel. He lowered his chin and begged. "Please, just wish me luck. I'm only looking for some laughs." He looked at the ground; Winston knew better than anybody how unhappy Avi had been. Some of their brethren committed suicide out of sheer depression.

Winston stepped to the side. "Go. Have fun. Tell Miller I said hi." Avi thanked him with a nod and trotted to the landing.

A half-hour later, he had reached Miller's hotel. The guy's flight arrived at noon and he asked Avi to come by at eight for dinner. On the drive to into downtown, Jersey had called, just checking in. The man's first few sentences alerted Avi that Win had called and given him the plan for the night—at least as he saw it. Jersey hadn't offered any disparaging remarks. He wished Avi a nice evening and was gone. *He's probably happy the guy's out of his hair…* Avi mused. Jersey had stolen away and then married Simon's beautiful wife. No wonder Jersey wanted the man distracted and in another state.

Jersey handed his keys to the valet, assuming he and Miller would take a car, and a swankily-dressed doorman swished open the glass entrance to the luxury hotel. Miller was standing in profile at the concierge station, signing autographs. Simon played pro-baseball and most humans thought he was very good at it. Avi didn't follow sports; he hung back to wait. Miller completed the task, ruffed the kid's hair, and shook Dad's hand in a business-like fashion. The pair left the opposite way and Simon raised his eyes to Avi's.

"Hey!" he said with more enthusiasm than Avi expected. The man said a parting word to the concierge and crossed the lobby to Avi's position. "So, you hungry? You look good. This is fun—I haven't been to Buffalo in ages."

Avi returned his energy, mentally erasing all the angst he had worked up the hours building up to the evening. Simon Miller chose the gourmet restaurant attached to his hotel and congenially led Avi with a hand to his elbow. He spoke all the way to the hostess stand and when the woman turned to find them a table, the man finally grew quiet.

"I had two espressos an hour ago," he said as an apology, turning to look Avi in the face. "I thought I'd look too tired after the flight."

"You look fantastic," Avi said, sensing he'd been fishing. He did, too. Taller by an inch, very blond with blue eyes and a camera-ready face—Simon had wowed Avi from the first time they met. The circumstance had been less than ideal, but the guy was handsome. And despite no longer being a Cow, he was drawn to the brethren. Avi wasn't classically attractive like Jersey or Beryl, but Simon was looking at him with an open and interested expression.

"What?" Avi said to Simon, drawing a hand down his face.

Simon looked away. "No, sorry," he said in a laugh. He guarded his lips and whispered, "I don't see any of you guys anymore. I sorta forgot how, well, you know."

Avi shot him a grin. "Not even Javier?" he asked, aware that both were followers of God. But Simon shrugged.

"I'm on the road and he's married." Simon hushed as a server arrived and led them to a table. When seated and menus dropped off, both men fell into discussing anything except Rakum, Cows, and married friends who left them behind.

An hour later, Simon pushed away from the table and laughed with his hands over his middle. "I'm not eating again for a year."

Avi grinned with him, not as full, but he'd never developed much of an appetite. Being mortal didn't mean "feeling" human. He had learned from the chatrooms that plenty of his brethren had trouble eating, sleeping, even fucking since becoming mortal. "It is what it is" didn't always cut it, either. He knew of several seeing human counselors for their anxiety.

"Come on—" Simon reached forward and playfully slapped his upper arm. "I know that look. Let's go to the bar—a little spirits for your spirit is all you need."

Avi forced a smile; he did feel better when looking at the man's face. He followed to the bar across the hotel complex, making small-talk about Winston's car fetish. Once seated at a small table, Simon asked what he did to pass the time.

"Jersey said before---you know---you were the inventor among them. Do you still do any of that?"

Avi laughed by surprise. Jersey's memory was fine, but the timing of that hobby had been a century ago, when technology needed his superior intelligence. "Sorry, didn't mean to laugh. I used to come up with all sorts of great mechanical shortcuts, even before your people had them—I invented a few things the mortals use even today. But… in the New World, I mostly wander around."

"Wandering while wondering what to do now?" Simon asked

with a smile. "You could go on the road with me. It's boring and I hate my teammates more than they hate me."

"You serious?" Avi asked.

"Yes, I hate them," Miller joked and nodded. "Yeah, lots of the guys bring a friend or girlfriend." His eyes flashed. "Don't get any ideas—I remember what happened that last time."

Avi wrinkled his nose. "No, you don't remember, remember? You had to ask Jersey."

"Haha," Simon laughed with a nod. "But, sure. My next tour is in three weeks. Just think about it."

Avi changed the subject and ordered another round. He wanted Simon drunk and so far, he was holding his whiskey better than Avi. When it grew close to midnight, Simon knocked back his most recent shot and grew quiet, staring into Avi's face. He still wasn't intoxicated, *at least not enough,* Avi added internally with a slightly guilty chuckle.

"I guess I'm really, really, really good at reading you guys's faces by now," he said to Avi, maybe slurring a little. Simon lowered his voice to a whisper although no other patrons were nearby. "Let's go up to my room—I'm not scared of you. Come on," he said and stood to his feet. "I have a mini-bar and…" he shrugged, "…we'll have a nightcap." Avi rose and agreed; he was drunk. He said so and Simon laughed without turning, leading the way out of the dark room.

On the elevator, Simon leaned back against the metal wall and considered Avi, his eyes at half-mast. "I'm sorry I'm not gay," he said as if truly apologizing. "I'd go after you if I was, honest."

Avi was about to blow off the topic when the car stopped and two men stepped on, assuming the right of the space when Avi hemmed closer to Simon on the left. One man's eye flicked their way and standing three-quarters behind him, Simon wrapped a thick forearm about his throat and pulled him into his body, both of them facing the strangers.

"Hands off, assholes," he said to their faces with no evident humor. Avi assumed they recognized the drink was talking because they snickered and faced front, mumbling low to each other. Simon came closer and spoke in his ear from behind. "See, scared 'em off you. I'd be good at this."

Avi agreed with a weak chuckle, not sure being good at "being gay" was what he wanted from Simon or anyone, for that matter. With mortals, a label was required for every little thing they did and said. A Rakum simply did what pleased him—no need to call it anything except pleasure, pain, work, or servitude—whatever a brother did, he did. The end.

"Here," one of the men said then, flicking a small white card to Avi who took it. It read across the front, "London Jigg" and two addresses, one in Buffalo on the eastside and the other in Hamburg, Germany. The man said no more and Avi flipped it to the back. A very attractive male-female couple graced the back, professional actors by the look. He raised his eyes to the stranger who faced away as the car slowed and stopped at his floor.

"What?" Avi asked. "London Jigg?" he said open-ended.

The second man turned to face him and number one left the elevator. This one was dashing, dressed in high style with feathered hair dyed a soft lavender. He met Avi's eye and gestured for the card. "Mr. Jigg is the most prolific manager of fashion models in the Free World. You have a look we need. Go to the website, see if its something you want to investigate." The man offered a little shrug and stepped out, his cohort already out of sight. "He has already hired you, so all you need do is show up at that address at any time."

The man raised his phone a millisecond and Avi heard a shutter click.

"If you show up, they will call Mr. Jigg."

Avi wiggled free of Simon and put one foot onto the floor to hold the door. "What's your name?"

The man hummed, looked at Simon still against the back wall, and then gave Avi a tight grin. *"You* can call me Jimmy. That one can't call me at all."

Avi didn't smile, but his eyes did. "Jimmy, I'm a millionaire and I'm bored as hell." He flicked his head the way the other man exited. "Is this modeling schtick fun?"

Jimmy glanced around Avi in an obvious manner and then met his eye once more. "Are you seriously going up with this guy? Come with us—I'll tell you all about it. Mr. Jigg has some clients in the Penthouse suite right now waiting for him. You can be our Plus-One."

Avi shook his head and peeked back at Simon. "Are you blind?"

Jimmy paused, his expression lax, then he took another look at Simon over Avi's shoulder and sighed. "Tomorrow, then. But not until noon." He flicked out a new card, this one bright neon green with purple lettering. "And if this doesn't pan out," he said with an eye-raise to Simon, "come to the Penthouse. I'll show them your pic."

Avi pocketed his card and backed into the elevator. Simon again pulled him close with his pitching arm, thicker than Avi had noticed the last time they met. The car started again, their floor one down from the penthouse.

"I wouldn't have let that guy steal you away," Simon said low, slurring more than before. "You Rakum are bad-ass and you could kill any of us, but I could completely own that pansy asshole right there. His master, too."

Avi pat Simon's arm below his chin. "It sounds like you think I'd sleep with that guy." Avi huffed. "You don't know me yet, Simon."

Simon hummed, his lips against Avi's ear. "I don't mind learning some new things," he said and the door opened on Simon's floor.

Avi swallowed and didn't speak to his friend's double-entendre, even though the man definitely meant it both ways. "You're in twenty-two?" he asked Simon who still hadn't released him and walked him bodily off the elevator and into the hallway. "Am I holding you up? Can you walk?" Avi asked him and he mumbled and laughed.

When they reached the correct door, Simon opened it with his thumbprint. Inside, the lights increased slowly to a romantic haze, the room consumed with a double-king bed and full-size onyx black armoire.

"Is this the honeymoon suite," he asked Simon with humor, but his friend only stepped him to the edge of the bed, released Avi's neck and flopped onto the bed on his front. "Are you asleep?" Avi asked and poked his side with one finger. Simon didn't respond and Avi poked him again, harder. "Simon?"

Ten seconds clicked by and Avi looked around the room. If Simon was asleep... He looked back to the door. He could join Jimmy in the Penthouse, see what that's all about. When he faced front again, Simon had rolled onto his back, his knees bent with both feet on the floor, and he was looking into Avi's face.

"Do you think Jersey wanted to sleep with me back then?" he asked clearly.

"Sure," Avi said easily. It had been a dumb question...

"And Beryl? We got really close after 11/13. Did he want to sleep with me, too?" Simon lifted his arms and propped his head onto his hands.

Avi didn't answer, having not been there and he had never known the twins well.

"I don't think he did," Simon said thoughtfully after another second. "I tried to reconnect after that crazy doctor poisoned me, Beryl stayed with me until I was well enough to go home, but... he's mad at me, I guess." Simon sighed and flicked his eyes to the space beside him. "Sit down. Are you leaving?"

Avi licked his lips. No, he wasn't leaving; Simon's body was speaking a language he read clearly. "Scoot up—" he shooed Simon with both hands. "Scoot up to the pillows."

With a humph of effort, Simon lifted both feet—boots and

all—and kicked his way across the thick duvet until his head reached the front sham. "Like this?"

Avi nodded and clambered onto the bed, crawling on his knees to meet Simon in the middle.

Simon held himself up on both elbows, watching Avi's activity.

"Go ahead. Lean back," Avi instructed and with a single raise of his brow, he sighed into the pillows. Avi maneuvered closer until in place and he reached for Simon's outside wrist. "Put your hand here," he said and brought the man's hand to his left cheek. "And close your eyes." Avi waited for him to do it, but Simon only grinned.

"I don't need step-by-step instructions," he dead-panned. "Just say, 'pretend I'm a woman.'" With a half-grin, Simon waited to see Avi's reaction.

"Oh, the naivete of you humans," he lamented with humor. He leaned in and touched his lips to Simon's, who'd been expecting him, mouth parted, ready to learn something new, as he had said. Avi kissed him, but not too deeply, and sensed Simon trying to do it correctly. "This is not a test and remember, you're not gay," Avi whispered and Simon closed his eyes to smile with chagrin.

After several minutes, Simon pushed him an inch away to catch his breath. He was smiling and laughing, blushing with one hand headed for his fly. "I think you're going to kill me with lust," he said laughing at his own words. Avi said nothing and helped him free his belt. "If I live through this, I don't want you to go on tour with me," he whispered, eyes still closed. "I might forget..." His voice trailed off but Avi understood.

He didn't want to be gay, turn gay, have gay trysts. He wanted his God, his job, his life, his daughter, maybe a new wife one day. Simon wanted one night—one night to figure out what the Rakum who had been chasing him wanted all this time. It was about the Rakum—Avi got it. The same went for him—Avi could sleep with any of the brethren he chose, they'd receive him, but a beautiful former Cow? He was using Simon just as much.

Deciding the conversation should cease for good, Avi grabbed the back of Simon's neck firmly, his hand aggressively gripping him through his jeans as well. Simon's eyes flew open, but he was smiling.

"This is it. And it's a one-off, so shut up and enjoy the ride. Got it?" In response, Simon reached for Avi's face and pulled him close.

Blind Date with a Hottie
Avi Meets Hester

"Come here," Winston said sternly as Avi crossed through to the kitchen.

Avi ignored him and continued on to dig through the refrigerator. Three weeks had passed since his date with Simon and as he had predicted—and desired, if the truth be known—it had been a one-time thing. Miller did not try to contact him and Avi hadn't been drawn to do so either. From the den, he heard Winston deliver the same command a second time with more fire in his tone.

With a sigh, he grabbed two bottles of water and headed back. He reached the recliner where his roommate sat and handed one over. "I'm fine. You can put the consoling lover schtick away."

"Lover? Shit," he chuckled, but said no more. Ten days ago, he'd consoled Avi the only way he knew how, so the label fit. "You need to stop drag-assing around. I think I might kill you in your sleep if you don't break out of this whatever it is."

Avi slumped into the neighboring loveseat with drama. "I'm open to ideas. I've tried just about everything."

"I might have an idea," Winston said and waited for Avi to show his interest. "I set you up on a blind date. It's tonight." He held up his hand when Avi looked like he would object. "He's a brother, you don't know him, and he and you have a lot in common."

"Like what?" Avi asked, as interested as he was suspicious.

"Like drag-assing around and driving his roommates nuts." Winston fiddled with his cell and flashed the screen to Avi. "I'll withhold his name for my own reasons, but, what do you think?"

Avi sniffed once and reached for the phone. Winston released it and Avi leaned back considering the face. The brother was a ginger, orange-red hair, a three-day beard and the pale skin his coloring brought, also, he was stunningly perfect in his features. His blue eyes popped right out of the 2D photo and even though only his neck and shoulders of his body were visible, he was obviously lithe, built like a dancer. The corner of Avi's mouth went up and Winston snatched it back with a laugh.

"Turned you on, eh?" he said and texted the picture to Avi. "He had the same reaction to your photo, so I guess it's kismet." Winston looked much to cheery, but Avi didn't ponder it. Instead, he opened his new texts and studied the man's face. "He'll meet you at The Pelican at eight. Said he'd wait in the lobby and I made you a reservation."

"Who's his Elder?" Avi asked, listening, but also growing painfully interested in the details.

"Ask him tonight. He's coming just as blind."

"Good game," Avi said absently and rose to get a shower.

His blind date was waiting in the lobby as promised, leaning casually against the wall, his face away from the door. He turned his head when Avi entered. *"Kazak,* brother," he said in a smooth accentless voice.

"Kazak," Avi returned. *"Polfasz, ke re hangfy."* (Our brothers have done a good thing).

At his observation, the redhead smiled, showing white teeth and dimples. Avi melted; this one had been *ish-mikhan* and inwardly, he shook his fist at Winston for not warning him.

"Name's Hester," the guy said and waited for Avi to close the distance, which he did, stopping a few feet away. "You're taller than I expected."

Avi grinned. He was six feet nothing and Hester looked to be a tiny bit shorter. Most brothers were taller but *it is what it is* and Hester might have been thinking the same tenet. He grinned then and stepped in to cup Avi's neck. He pulled him close and kissed his jaw.

"You smell nice, too," Hester said when stepping back.

Avi was thrilled to be welcomed in a familiar way. Since their way of life died out, the brethren didn't know how to act around each other. Having Hester treat him in the Old Way gave him comfort and he numbly pointed to the hostess stand.

Once seated, Hester leaned over folded arms and relaxed with an exhale. He held Avi's gaze and the silence was comfortable. After a few moments, his mouth turned into a secret grin and he licked his lips. "You start," he said and his boyish face shined.

Avi nodded with a matching wry grin. "Born in 1878, assigned to Elder Tomás, who I served until the Last Assembly. After that, Winston's been my compatible the past fifty years. It's been weird between us since 11/13 and he makes friends more easily with mortals. My skill was cognitive, so I've been a scientist and inventor. How about you?" Avi asked and then huffed. "Besides the obvious."

"Is it obvious?" he asked with a new smile. "If you'll just tell me how pretty I am."

He raised his eyebrows and Avi discerned he meant it. Avi leaned close and spoke in his ear. "My entire body is humming like a livewire since we locked eyes. So yes, you are gorgeous and it's killing me."

Hester grinned with a nod and remained close, leaning in. "Fantastic. We'll get along just fine."

"I think so, too," Avi whispered.

It wouldn't take much to cause their lips to meet, at the table, in front of the entire establishment. Hester beat him to it. By simply releasing the air from his lungs, his brother was in contact, his lips hot and as soft as butter. He didn't use his tongue, rather by allowing their lips to press without tightness, Avi had a sense of melting into one creature. His head swam as his internal clock ticked the seconds. Only when a server passed and dropped off their water glasses did Hester break it off. He remained close, inches away, his eyes flicking from Avi's and back to his lips again.

"Why are we here? This mortal dating is shit," Hester whispered, his gaze locked with Avi's. "I want to fuck—why are we here? You so hungry?"

Avi flushed. "We're mortal, Hester. Shouldn't we adopt their ways?"

"They do this," he said with a wicked grin. "Let's be the sort that fall in love at first sight and fucks that very hour. That's the sort of mortal I'll be. Let's you and me be that couple so hot they can't stop fucking."

Avi swallowed, his will already dissolved when Hester first smiled. "Where shall we go?" he rasped, his throat suddenly dry.

Hester glanced about the romantically-lit dining area, his eyes landing on the Lavatories sign. "There," he said with a dip of his chin. "And then my place." He reached for Avi's thigh under the table. "And then your place, and then any place we like."

Avi stood. Hester did, too, and his hand landed on Avi's midback as they began their walk to the restrooms. His new friend was exactly right—humans were notoriously impetuous. Now he and Hester could be human together. This perfect man thought Avi was handsome and sexy—*I'll no longer be lonely,* he thought happily. Things were surely looking up.

"Wait, you didn't tell me you lived with Jersey," Hester said propping onto one elbow to look upon Avi's face. He remained reclined on the futon, eyes closed, as happy and comfortable as he'd been since 11/13.

"What should I say?" he responded, truly with nothing to add.

Jersey made the misery of the post-apocalypse bearable, the end.

"Well," Hester said and chose his words. "how many other *ish-mikhan* have you bedded?"

Avi peeked out one eye to see Hester's expression. Was he jealous? Or curious as to how he stacked up?

"How many?" Hester pressed.

"In 1972, a fix-it man named Julio gave me a blowjob. Like that, you mean?" Avi asked now opening both eyes since his friend's tone had grown harsh.

"Julio…" Hester said with a slow nod. "And that's it? Julio and Jersey."

"And Hester," Avi finished for him waiting to see his direction.

"Huh," was all he remarked after a long silence.

Avi threw him a bone. "It's completely different with you." He sat up and propped against the pillows, crossing his arms over his middle. "After 11/13, Winston and I moved out of Jersey's place and stopped sleeping together. We messed around here and there, but it wasn't – it isn't – the same now that we're human."

"Jersey's not as good?" Hester asked and Avi felt he now understood the line of questioning.

"*Nothing* is as good, you know it's not. Food tastes like shit, bruises take forever to heal, and orgasms last milliseconds." He shrugged as he stopped with the examples. Hester knew all this but seeing him nod in agreement helped anyway. "Hester," he said making sure he had his eye, "you're an amazing lover. I want to see you again, do this a lot, get to know you better."

Hester was listening but looked as if he wanted to interject. Avi asked him to do so and he sighed.

"I never slept with Jersey but I had to follow him my entire life."

Avi nodded once. "Ahh, and our brethren compared your services?" Hester huffed. "To your face?"

"Not directly, but any mention of Jersey, oblique or not, while

I'm jerking a brother off isn't fun to hear."

"I don't see how you two compare," Avi said and opened his arms to caress Hester's near bicep. "I didn't think about Jersey at all until just now—since I met you for dinner, he never crossed my mind."

Hester smiled, small and human, his eyes softening. He licked his lips. "So that's why you didn't tell me you and Winston lived with him—because you have all the *ish-mikhan* you need right here, right now."

Avi tugged his arm, inviting him to lower and he did. After a lengthy kiss, Hester lay down again, spooning against Avi one arm across his chest. "Let's do this. Let's just stay together until we make each other sick."

"Yeah," Avi said and wondered if that could ever happen. If they were going to be mortal together, maybe they would stay tight. Or… "Do you think being a fix-it man will keep you from settling down?"

Hester seemed to be pondering the question and finally sighed. "It seems likely. I only know how to do one thing really, really well. I only enjoy that one thing. Eventually, I'll need a new person to do it with. Make sense?"

Avi agreed with a small sound. "Then let's hope it takes a long time to figure out ol' Avi."

Hester lifted to see his face and gave him a devastating smile. "You have yourself a deal. So kiss me, handsome."

Avi's favorite phrase.

Rafael
Tall, Latino, & Thick in the Right Places

Ten months later, the rose had lost its bloom.

Tonight, they shared a pizza with Winston and his girl, who saw them as an adorable gay couple, as normal as any she knew in her college classes. Avi enjoyed that part of the game—pretending to be progressive and militant about the issues important to the LGBTQ+ community. Winston's date probed them both about how the locals received their "queerness." Before 11/13, none of that stuff mattered, but every day (if not every hour), Avi became more and more aware of how important it was to humans to label everything in their lives. *I mean, shit, she had named her car.* When the pizza was devoured and conversation lulled, Win took her away and Hester and Avi headed home.

In the car, Hester lobbed insults regarding Avi's driving skills, always laughing it off as a joke. Avi was still Rakum enough to strike out if he went too far, and Hester had learned this. Still, he knew how to bat his eyelashes, pucker up, and force Avi to forgive him using skill honed over a century of intense study.

Now they were alone in their new apartment and Avi's mind turned to the old days. Or more precisely, the days before he met Hester. Back when he lived with Winston and tolerated his old roommate's various sexual encounters.

"Tell me about your first lover," Hester said, relaxing on the short sofa stretched out with one foot to the floor and the other heel on the opposite arm.

Avi swiveled his attention and considered possible responses. He didn't want to notice his housemate's allure, but damn. It didn't matter how weary the guy made him in the day-to-day; when he put the smolder in his gaze, Avi stiffened. Like Jersey, the man never lost an ounce of appeal.

"I don't have a first lover," Avi answered finally and wrenched his gaze to the phone in his hand. He scrolled pages with his thumb and Hester cleared his throat.

"You know what I mean, asshole. Who was the first brother you *wanted*? The first guy to get you hard all by himself."

"Why?" Avi said under his breath pretending to read. Truly, he was seeking an answer. He had been slender, handsome, agreeable—just the sort of grunt a senior Rakum might like to have in his lap. But when he was old enough to choose for himself?

"Who was it?" Hester pressed and made a big show of raising both arms up and behind his head. Avi only watched peripherally, happy the guy was still dressed. Hester kicked off his shoes and Avi turned his head to see what else might come off. Hester smiled and remained, the back of his head propped on his hands.

"Why don't you tell me yours while I think about it," Avi said, his eyes returning to his phone.

"The question doesn't apply to *ish-mikhan*, idiot," Hester said in a soft voice, his insult sounding like an endearment. "We want to see everyone's eyes big. But you… I'm interested. You left your lair house and went to your first Elder. You were in his company when you came of age, so… who was it?" Hester paused until Avi looked over. He shot him another sweet smile at the eye lock. "Or was it one of them? A mortal? Was it a woman?"

"No, it was a brother," Avi said and his mind traveled back. He exhaled when the full memory rolled in, yet he still didn't feel like playing Hester's game.

"Who?" Hester said, this time in a whisper. He sat up in a smooth movement, paused a second or two and then stood to take the three steps to Avi's recliner. He sat halfway on the armrest and dropped his hand to Avi's shoulder. "Do I know him?"

"Rafael," Avi said in the same whisper. He looked up and to

his left and Hester squeezed his fingers with a grin.

"Rafa, Rafa, touch me there!" he cooed in a heavy breath. "Oh, he was handsome. How did it happen? Were you alone?"

Avi grinned despite himself. Yes, the man was eye candy, but masculine and hard. He was much older, he preferred women, and he didn't mess around with the brethren unless instructed to do so. The game began to feel like fun. Avi pictured the Rakum in question, 6'3", dark, Latino, thick where he needed to be, eyes so black...

"Your face," he said and dropped the contact to run his fingers into Avi's short hair, falling into a gentle scalp massage that caused Avi's eyes to go to half-mast. Shit, he'd tell it all, the promise of a special Hester-reward growing every moment.

"I ran the pack's courier service; one night, on an unfamiliar route, I found myself…" Avi grinned as he sought the correct term.

"You got lost," Hester said and Avi shrugged one shoulder. "This was what? 1960?"

"Yeah, San Diego. I sent out a beacon. There were two packs nearby besides my own and the first man to answer was Rafa."

Hester sighed a giddy noise and moved his mass across Avi's lap, one arm about his shoulders, sitting like a huge child. Avi smiled, too, for many reasons.

"Rafa had a fun job—he scoured the bars and clubs for consenting females. His master sent him out several times a week with the instruction to return with a woman to screw and drink."

"Great job for Rafa," Hester offered.

"He had been only a block away and we met at the nearest corner." Avi recalled everything with such detail and he grinned anew. In his lap, Hester grew shorter of breath, his excitement building with the tale. The night was going to end well and Avi continued the story with more vigor. "It was 2 AM and he had just returned from delivering a woman to his master so he was freed up. He liked my face, he told me so, said I looked friendly—like a Cow he kept across town. I didn't care for the comparison at the time, but he launched into explaining how it was a compliment, that Cows were special and worthy, blah blah blah. I nodded my head and agreed, something about his voice…"

"That accent," Hester said and hushed, waiting for more.

"Yeah, and combined with his sinewy movement and height and at one point, we were strolling shoulder to shoulder down the dark sidewalk and he asked where I was spending the day."

"Shit…"

Avi grinned. "He helped me find the address I sought and once I had the package, he showed me to his place."

Hester was smiling, but his head went side to side. "I wonder what made him suddenly want to take you to bed."

Avi chewed his lip and huffed. "At the point where he invited me to sleep over, he probably only wanted a blowjob. But we continued to talk, I made him laugh. He thought I was hilarious, which none of my brothers agreed with. Once we made it to his apartment, he owned the building, four floors and a finished basement. He rented the top four and his area had hidden doors and no human access. It was sweet."

"I wish I had seen that."

"Inside, he asked me about my pack and seemed to be talking a lot more than any brother I had ever known. He talked me right into his bedroom, on and on and on, asking me everything he could think of. When he removed his shoes and then his shirt…"

"Oh, shit," Hester whispered and ran his fingers into Avi's shirt between the buttons. "He had the hairiest chest."

Avi grinned with a nod. "He said he discerned I was ready and said he wanted me to pretend he wasn't my superior. *'We're the same age, same rank, our masters want us to spend the day together. What should we do now?'* just like that."

"You said…" Hester whispered, his hand returning to Avi's scalp, the slow circles calming and exciting at the same time.

"I said, okay, equal brother, let me see the rest." Avi laughed and Hester did, too. Rafael had grinned, a devastating sparkle in his dark eyes, and 100-year-old Avi watched his fingers unbuckle the leather belt to disrobe.

"Okay, and you got to practice on him what your brethren practiced on you for decades," Hester stated in a chuckle meant to be derisive, but Avi didn't care. He'd been with the man long enough that his passive-aggressive style of foreplay drummed up no angst. "What did you do first?"

Avi kicked the recliner back and as his upper body relaxed Hester had to rebalance on his lap. Avi grasped Hester's forearm and tugged. "I'll show you, come close."

Hester offered resistance but then dropped forward until he lay mostly atop Avi on the chair. "I didn't sleep with him," he said in a soft voice and Avi figured he meant he'd only serviced the guy. Get him off and move on to the next, which was the norm for an *ish-mikhan* at work. It might be fun to hear a blow-by-blow (haha) account of their brief moment, but it could turn Hester's mood.

"He missed out," Avi said low and waited for Hester to look at him again. When their eyes met, his roommate was ready to start his engines. Between kisses and caresses, he gave Hester a detailed account of his long winter's day underground with the beautiful and sexy Rafael of Elder Blu's pack. A tiny cursor in the back of his mind reminded Avi that when the two of them had showered and dressed and faced a new day, they'd be fighting again. Somehow, that mattered less than nothing as long as his tongue was hot and his hands gentle. Tomorrow was a million years away.

The next section is a memory Avi revealed to me, not Hester.
~ Jersey

1960, that same night in San Diego. Sundown.
Avi awoke first but didn't leave the bed. A low-wattage bulb in the adjacent bath provided enough illumination to admire his new friend's physique. Rafa outweighed him by forty pounds, that

being taut muscle across his entire frame. Every Rakum developed into whatever their DNA allowed, without special diets or exercise regimens, each man simply grew into their best form by the age of seventy. Avi didn't mind—all the brethren were beautiful in their own way and this time he had attracted one that suited his maturing tastes.

"I wonder why I can't see your thread," Rafa said then in his killer accent, his eyes closed facing upwards.

Avi made a small humph and settled onto his back to ponder. What Rafael meant was he couldn't read his mind—he'd be able to see any brother's surface thoughts but going deeper took special training. Master Tomas taught him a few tricks to the mystical gift of telepathy, so he saw Rafa's thread, though faintly.

"I felt you watching me, though," he continued a small grin hitting his mouth. After another long moment, he sighed and sat up, swinging his feet to the floor, his long back to Avi. "I hear my Cow, Pedro." The outer doorbell sounded and Rafa stood. "Let's go up and see him. He'd enjoy meeting you."

Avi rose and reached for his jeans, wondering at the man's affectionate tone toward a mortal. He didn't care for them as a rule and a Cow? Well, they were especially low.

"I think you enjoyed Rafa, si?" he said watching Avi dress. He wore only his boxers for the moment and he crossed strong arms at his chest. "This Cow, Pedro, he has a wife. He loans her out to me. Tonight, you have her. Brand new stone should have a woman, too."

Avi made a neutral face and as he buttoned his shirt, Rafa finally began to don his slacks. "I've bedded women," he told him, although the number of females he'd prodded was two, and both of those on orders from Elder Tomas. When a female angered their master, he sent her to be ravaged by whoever was around. Avi had been home two of those instances.

"No, you've raped them," Rafa said with a *tsk*. "Marisol will show you how to romance a woman. Trust me, it is a good lesson.

Good to possess these skills."

Avi shrugged. None of the men in his pack were tender with women and his mind sought why they should be. He didn't want to ask, but his new friend *tsked* again.

"I am 250 years old and over my lifetime, my master has ordered me to cajole females 427 times. If I didn't know how to make love, I would have failed him 427 times." Rafa watched for Avi to agree.

"I hadn't thought of that. My master isn't inclined that way," he said after a pause. Rafael sighed with what sounded like irritation and then stepped around the bed to stand before Avi.

"Are you going to trust me on this?" he asked, his black eyes deep and holding Avi with tenacity. Deep inside, a yearning began to grow and Avi swallowed. In a sudden but smooth motion, Rafa lifted one hand to Avi's cheek, gently cupping it in his palm. "You give it your all tonight and return home with me for the day." He dropped his volume and the guttural baritone further stoked Avi's newfound flame. "Stay in my bed and tell me all about it."

A slow grin hit Avi's mouth. "I like this plan."

Rafa smiled in his space and dropped his hand. "Then come. Pedro grows impatient. He was born into my service as was his father before him. He and Marisol are trying to conceive a son for me to continue with. If there is time, taste Pedro's blood and you will know why I keep him close."

Avi trailed Rafa to the hidden exit, one hand to his gut. He hadn't had solid food in more than 24 hours so drinking the man's blood would be especially intoxicating. When they reached an exterior wall panel that disguised a door, Avi touched Rafa's back to have him pause. He turned with upraised brow.

"Will Marisol consent her blood?" he asked.

"No, she can't bring herself to consent," Rafa replied with a sorrowful expression. "She has tried, but it sours. It's no Bueno."

Avi exhaled. "I will ask anyway," he said with a small shrug and Rafa grinned. He opened the passageway on silent hinges and before long, they crept upon Pedro, his back turned, and waiting for his master by the fire.

A half-hour later, Avi led newly introduced Marisol to an unoccupied bedroom. She was beautiful, thirty, full-figured, with skin as soft as butter, and long ebony hair that flowed down her back like an onyx river. He had heard Rafael's instructions to her before they left the great room—*"Will you show my brother how to love a woman? He is a virgin."*—and Avi played the part.

Marisol instructed him first how to kiss and where to place his hands while both parties were still clothed. Without any effort, his mind ticked the minutes, and they kissed and petted over their clothing for twelve and a half minutes. She moved them to the futon and with them both on their side facing one another, she showed him how to push beneath her underclothes and simply by mimicking what she did on her end, he met her movements equally. It was twenty-two minutes before they were both undressed and ready to copulate, and in another three, he was finished. She collapsed onto her back as if they had completed the act.

Sweating and smiling, Avi propped upon his elbow and looked down on her. "I've seen a few movies... you're supposed to come, too," he said looking into her dark eyes. She offered a tiny smile and guided his hand and then his movements to help her meet the same end.

When she was as tingly and he was, they both lay on their backs simply enjoying the afterglow. Before too long, a car horn outside broke the silence and Avi felt for her hand and wrapped his fingers in hers.

"Rafael told me that you don't consent your blood," he said in a romantic voice. In his peripheral vision, she turned her face to his profile. "I wish you could. I don't know if you realize how rare it is, how wonderful and heavenly..." Hoping the guilt trip worked, Avi laid it on thick, turning to see her face at the last word.

She swallowed and licked her lips, and looked to be thinking it over. Finally, she said in Spanish, "I will try."

Jersey propped up once more, brow lifted. "Say, I consent."

Marisol inhaled and then in a slow nod, she said, "Senor Avi, I consent."

Barely bottling his exuberance, Avi reached for his jeans still slung to the floor. He fished out his pocketknife and rejoined her position, leaning close. He kissed her lips, long and closed-mouthed and moved the contact from her jaw, her throat, and down her arm, feeling for the vein closest to the skin in her wrist. So far, her heart-rate was steady, so far, it looked good. Rafa indicated that in the past, she consented and recanted before the deed was completed. Avi had made the puncture and his tongue went to catch the first drop. If she changed her mind...

Shit shit shit shit! Avi's inner mind shouted as the food of the gods hit his palate. She hadn't chickened out and her blood absorbed into his system like quicksilver. If his orgasm had been delightful, the buzz related to her consenting blood offer was exponentially more. He stopped himself before thirty seconds elapsed and covered the wound tightly with one hand, seizing with his eyes squeezed closed. Marisol was still and when he tucked his head down and his face into her breasts, she wrapped her outside arm about his head and kissed his hair. It was three minutes before the effects allowed him to uncurl his body and he collapsed onto his back laughing with joy. Marisol commented on his erection and he took her on round two. When he saw Rafael an hour later, he had a fantastic story to tell and had left his new friend with the greatest gift of all—because of tonight, Marisol no longer feared giving blood to the Rakum; Rafa had a female blood donor. A thing so rare.

It is appropriate to end my rebuttal with a chapter
written entirely by Darcy Vandiver.
Go ahead, polcz-v'…
~ Jersey

Darcy & the CEO
Bonding with the Boss

Year 2020

When Winston asked me up for a visit, I asked him to shoot straight regarding *why*. I had already proved to him when we were last together that I do what I want and if I want to fuck, I will. If he wanted me up there for my expertise in bed, be up front. Then I could decide if I wanted the same thing. I had no doubt we'd dance naked if I came, I just couldn't allow Win—or anyone—to ever feel they one-upped Darcy Vandiver.

"Look, Darss," he said in his put-on southern accent, "Seven of our brothers meet here once a month for cards, whoring, whatever. We drink, we laugh, we go to the fight club, we have fun. Two of the brethren know you from your days with Elder Pebb…"

"Names," I said expecting the story to grow interesting. So far, I was bored to death. I run a busy construction company and spend my free time chasing tail or sneaking to Jersey's for beers (and whatever that leads to) when his wife is away.

"Tarn and Gilmore. I bragged on you last month and they both fell out of their seats with excitement—they were pitiful." Win barked a few chuckles.

"When do I need to be there?" No need to say more. Unlike some Rakum, I recall much of my past and these two had been extremely compatible bunkmates. For reference, it was not uncommon for Master Pebb to call all three of us simultaneously. We worked that well together. It's a good memory, all of it.

163

Winston railed off the deets and I asked about Avi. I hadn't bedded the guy, but he was good to Jersey many years and I wanted to pay my respects.

"I'll invite him. He got a place with Hester across town."

"Shit," I said laughing. If you knew Hester, you'd laugh, too.

Once I hung up, I rang Jersey to see if he wanted to come along. At the penning of this chapter, he's married with two children and one on the way. (I was kidding earlier, LM. Jersey and I are just bros now). In fact, I still sleep with whomever I want, but my eye is out for a wife life-mate. I want a little woman cooking me dinner with a tiny Darcy inside. Yeah, I'm not modern and whoever I end up with will know it. ANYWAY, Jersey was headed out of town with the fam, so I went back to work.

It's a busy time. I'm hiring a new CEO to handle firing and hiring over the next few months. I like to scramble the eggs when they get too individualized. My Board brought my numbers sky-high the first three quarters and I was happy. I don't go to the office, I'm the boss, I show up now and then to start shit and try to catch someone screwing in the supply room. When I showed up three weeks back, two of my top guys (well, one's a woman) were driving Lamborghinis. I don't like that. Their income was sufficient, but a quick mental calculation told me that if they owned or leased a home, they'd be stretching their budget with such wheels. If they were bad stewards with their money, I couldn't let them handle mine, Pebb Construction (how's that for an homage?), a four billion-dollar multi-national corporation. So today, I was interviewing my choice for Chief Exec.

Bam-bam let the candidate in. I call her Bam-bam because of how she makes love. I think I've bedded all the women in my employ, and this one, my Executive Assistant will work under whomever I hire. Maybe they'll try out Bam-bam, too. He walked in and I pointed to the chair.

"This is it. You ready?" I asked him. He had to know he was hired; we had put him under a four-person panel interview, three department heads saw him individually, I sent him to Paris to meet the team there, and he had one with Baron, the only former Cow I have in my company. Side note, Baron and I have never been to bed. He repulses me. I didn't know him before 11/13 and wonder how any brother put their mouths on him. But, let's get back to the candidate.

"Yes, sir, I'm ready. You've chosen the right man for the job."

He sat in the wide office Queen Anne as if he owned the room. I liked that, knees slack and apart, elbows on the armrests with hands dangling without tension, and his head to the side. He was an alpha male and his resume paired with his persona said he could carry this company several quarters, maybe even years.

"Excellent," I said and stood up from around my desk. He stepped toward me, hand out to shake. His grip was firm, his hand not as big as mine, but he matched the measure of muscle I used in every man-to-man handshake. I had a sudden nutty thought. He wouldn't refuse so I ran it past my mind another few times before I said it aloud. "I have an inkling you might be the CEO this company needs for a long time. You could make a career here. Do your job well, and if ever another job looks better or you're offered more money, come to me and I'll top it. Do you believe me?"

Chief nodded. "You know I've worked as CEO for IBM and Southern Company, both companies I intended to stay but was bought away. I can say with all sincerity—if possible, I'd stay with Pebb till retirement."

He had answered perfectly for what I wanted to ask of him next. "The interview is over, but I want you to come with me on a little trip next weekend. The owner of this company wants a little bonding time. What do you say?"

I surprised him, his brows arched, but he recovered and chuckled. It was a good look for him, half-smile in that serious George Clooney face. I should mention, he doesn't actually resemble the actor, but he has that sort of swagger with an embrace of natural handsomeness, a "I can do anything I put my mind to and I don't give a shit about trivial issues" look. That's about how I feel, too.

"Just tell me what to pack," he said and gave my hand another firm pump. I sent him out to see Bam-bam for the details. My trip to New York had become much more interesting.

On the flight from Atlanta to LaGuardia, Chief (I'm withholding his name) answered probing questions about his childhood. Rakum didn't have a childhood and since we lost our birthright, I have grown increasingly interested in their little life stories. I should have been a psychiatrist because with no formal training in the field, I am able to dissect a mortal's past by his current behaviors. And if they share tiny details from their pasts, I can divine behaviors sure to appear as time barrels on. It turned out that Chief had been raised in an orphanage and adopted at age twelve by a Jewish couple in Brooklyn. He shared little things that didn't ruin a human child's psyche, things you could say aloud in a full jetliner. When we got inside the limo to take us to the hotel, I asked him more pointed questions regarding his sexual history. Is it any wonder an ish-mikhan would be most interested in this? A human man does not divulge closely-held private information unless he first hears a secret in payment, so I fabricated a few tales for him regarding my youth, that I had been raised by a single mother and when I was eleven, her boyfriend raped me. You know, stuff that might provoke him to admit such things to me, his new boss, paying him over a million a year, plus bonuses.

"Shit, man, that's bad," he said and sounded sincere. He swished a forlorn headshake but held my eye meaning he wasn't embarrassed for me and I tucked that info away. "I heard about guys getting diddled or groped by coaches or teachers, but I guess I lucked out."

I knew he was divorced with three children in college, but I asked a new question to provoke him. I enjoy that. I am what I am.

"Do you sleep with guys?" I liked that he wasn't offended. I've been on the planet long enough that I expect one of two reactions to that question. Chief had the right one.

"Not so far," he said with a chuckle that expressed he wasn't attracted to men but didn't want to offend his new boss if he happened to be. Smart.

I gave him a nod and leaned back to relax into the seat. "Tonight, we're invited to a private party. All men, and some of them might come on to you. These guys are family to me and mean no harm. All you have to do is say no."

"No problem," Chief said with a tip of his chin. He looked out the window on his side so I watched his profile as he continued. "I have some cousins who are gay and Sarah's first husband left her for a man." One shoulder made the tiniest micro-shrug, which I always notice. "I guess you'd say when my personality and sex drive were being formed, I had no one in that vein to model after. I made myself into the image of my father. He was a great man and I have always wanted to be like him."

I made a tiny huff and he looked over, brows up. "What you just said sounds like a Bible verse," I told him with a wave of my hand. "I didn't ask before, but are you religious?"

"Does it matter?" he asked and I realized he meant as an employee.

"No, you have the job, even if you're a nutcase Republican Conservative Fundamentalist Christian," I responded with a half-smile.

He returned a full grin and rest his hands in his lap, relaxed as usual. "Guilty." He laughed then and watched my face. I suppose my expression caused him to think I was unsure of him now because he added, "I promise not to spread Gospel tracts around the construction site. On my honor."

I laughed and told him that was smart thinking. The car was pulling up to the hotel entrance and Chief reached to the floorboard for his briefcase. When he was sitting upright again, our eyes locked.

"If you don't believe in God, that's not my business," he said without a hint of judgment in his tone. The driver opened the door as he shot me one more glance to end with, "the Puppeteer will have his way with us no matter what we think or say or do." And he stepped onto the sidewalk.

The Puppeteer.

Why would he say that? Why would he call the God of the mortals The Puppeteer? You see, my favorite master used that term for the Maker. To hear this erudite and successful alpha use that same term… That was when Chief went on my NTF list. And I put an asterisk by his name—make it this weekend.

Winston had purchased a ranch house on eleven acres and he sent a car to pick us up at the hotel after we had showered and had a bite to eat. Chief was fifty and so far, he seemed fit enough to hang all night with a posse of former bloodsuckers. Speaking of fitness, I had arranged for us to have adjoining rooms and once we had checked in and gone to our respective heads to piss, he rapped on the door between our rooms and said we should keep it open. I don't know if any of Jersey's readers get what that says to an ish-mikhan. Do they know what it says to a mortal boss-man who holds the man's job in his sweaty palms? Multiply that by a factor of ten.

Chief wanted me to come on to him.

Did he want to fuck? No, the invitation didn't say that, but it said he expected or at least would not be offended if his new boss ogled him a little. Trust me. I've been doing this for centuries.

So we had the door ajar and with me in my room and him in his, we cleaned up and groomed for a night out. I was dressed in dark blue bootcut jeans and a deep red pullover, ready to go in twenty minutes, and he stepped into the opening between the two rooms wearing old-man boxers.

"Oh, good," he said with a glance at my outfit. Then he turned away saying, "I didn't want us to be twins."

Fifty-years old and he looked really good. He had no abdomen definition, probably lost that when he stopped lifting weights, but at some point in his past he lifted a lot. The round and wide shoulders I noticed through his clothing were thick with muscle trained over decades. Biceps not cut, but bulging and pecs as perfectly formed as my own, only not hard as they must have been during his gym days. Whatever happens in a man's life that draws him away from the gym had happened to Chief, but none of that reduced my desire… no, my *need* to run my hand across his chest. Moving on.

Chief led the way to the elevator. He'd worn blue jeans, relaxed and well-worn-in, with work boots and a plaid dress shirt open two buttons. He looked like a CEO trying to look casual, and the funny thing? He was trying to look that way. He was playing a role for my brothers. I told him so in the elevator and he owned up.

"Yeah, I want to project exactly that—a stuffy businessman out for beers with the boss. A little nervous, a little unsure about the men he doesn't know, but hoping his overall performance impresses."

I got a really good laugh from that and clapped his shoulder. I gave him a word of advice before the door opened to the lobby. "For the rest of this trip, do not refer to The Puppeteer by that name," I said grinning and he matched my expression. "A very passionate part of my past used that term and when you say it, I get hard in all the right places. *Comprende?"*

I had used Elder Canaan's word, too, and actually did make my jeans a little snug. Chief nodded holding my eye. He believed me and he comprehended. I let it drop—if he got too close, he would be fucking Darcy Vandiver. As far as I am concerned, I warned him. His new boss likes men and may have taken a shine to his new CEO.

It took thirty minutes to reach Win's estate and Chief and I swapped war stories. I'd been playing with mortals long before we lost our mojo, as Jersey calls it, so I know how to turn my actual experiences into tales fit for human ears. I have extensive knowledge of other countries, so I described foreign military skirmishes I'd been in and he'd done some fighting in Iraq, regular army. Once the car stopped at an impressive two-story classic Ranch style home, we got out without the driver's assistance and headed up the walk. I had sent to Win's phone, *"+1 Pulgh osc'l'v"* (a mortal unaware of Rakum), so I wasn't surprised no one met us in the yard. They were probably inside planning how to act around Darcy Vandiver and now a mortal who knew nothing of their people. I grinned as I pushed open the door—this was precisely why I brought my CEO as a buffer.

"Kazak!" Tarn belted and jogged to meet me in the doorway. I hadn't even stepped across the threshold before he shouldered Chief aside and grabbed my neck. The squirt came up to my chin and to chap his ass I resisted his tug. He was in my eye and read I was being an asshole. He grinned and kissed what he could reach.

I moved him to my right and held him in place with an arm about his shoulders. I hadn't seen him since Assembly 1950, but it felt as if only a day had passed, so familiar we were. I positioned myself next to Chief and flopped my left arm on him the same way and faced the men looking at us from the main room.

"Kazak, brothers," I announced and then I said in Rakum Hungarian, "just use our language on private stuff." I introduced Chief for who he was and all the guys came forward. I hadn't met four of the seven present and Avi was not in sight. Gilmore, my other old Pebb bunkmate came close and Chief had stepped away to shake hands and make greetings. Being alone a moment, my old pal got the kiss he deserved and told me I looked better than ever. I get that a lot, and I appreciate it. I understand I'm aging now, so

I work on it.

The four brothers I hadn't met circled up and Tarn, Gilmore and Winston stayed back, engaging Chief in chatter. These guys were all from Fawn's pack and knew Winston since First Ritual. I won't belabor their descriptions because I can sum them up in one word: hungry. They had been soldiers in the Old Way, and they filled their nights with violence and blood. They mostly fucked each other and had no finesse with women. I read in their faces that being mortal hadn't lessened their Rakum drive for chaos and destruction. Once each man made small flirtations to me, complimenting me in whatever way they could imagine, they opened the ring for me to go into the big room.

Winston came up and waited for me to turn. He didn't make contact, which was wholly appropriate. I had thrown him a bone back then; we weren't familiar.

"You look well," he said low after a new kazak. "You're the guest of honor so what will it be?" His eyes flit to Chief and back. "The fight club has a few mortals, but they know us," he said in our language.

Chief looked over from his conversation with Tarn. I sent him a wink that said it's not important and he turned back.

"We have a few great clubs, a brothel, and right here a card game with all the booze, weed, and conversation you need." Win had given me the choices holding my eye. In the old days, I would have read his thoughts, but his eyes begged enough.

"The others have kissed me quite a lot in front of my straight CEO," I told him in Rakum Hungarian very low. "Now you want to kiss the fix-it man too?" Win's mouth made the tiniest grin. He wanted much more than a kiss.

The feeling and thought that hit me at that moment is the only reason I considered avoiding Win and Avi since the Last Battle. I wanted to turn back time, grab that asshole and yank him to the bedroom. Why? In a very short minute, we'd be done and the entire night lay ahead. What came from such an insignificant explosion of sensation? As a Rakum, we had no use for a clock. We avoided the sun but the rest of the minutes worked for us, not against. I would do the man, do maybe Tarn and Gilmore, and watch the others jerk each other off and we'd go find some Cows and drink as much blood as possible. All without a care.

Now?

I only wanted to see what Chief would do if presented with the opportunity to fuck his boss.

I checked my CEO's position and he was facing away, still talking with the others, and I gave Winston more kiss than he deserved. When I released him, his jeans tented and with a grin he excused himself.

To the room I announced, "Chief and I want to play cards. Poker. Set 'em up." I took my place beside my employee and we sat together at the table. I focused my attention on him over the next three hours of cards and drinks. Neither he nor I smoked or imbibed in narcotics, but a few of my brothers let loose and eventually came to blows, fussing over something stupid.

At 2 AM, Winston asked me privately to sleep over. I considered it—well, I considered slipping upstairs with him a few minutes and returning to take Chief back to the hotel. But then I'd smell like Winston—some cheap ass cologne that I did not care for. I told him in his ear, "I want to try out the Chief so save my place. I'll come by tomorrow night." I watched his eyes and he nodded, enjoying my consideration. In another few minutes, I led Chief to the door and he went to the car when I said I needed a moment to say goodbye.

Tarn and Gilmore kissed me too long, but I was behind the door, not wanting Chief to see too much of that stuff. Once I was in the car with him, we headed back and he didn't speak for a full minute. I didn't care, I had nothing to say, buzzing pleasantly on the last two shots of bourbon I'd nabbed before the goodbyes began. Chief still sat front-and-center on the F-list, but I could imagine falling asleep instead. Sometimes that happens now that

I'm mortal—a urge to snooze can overshadow a bang if the circumstances are right.

"The High Father didn't do that," Chief said in a low voice, not speaking to me, but to the air. That combination of words didn't fit in a human's mouth and my ears perked. Before Last Assembly, we had Ten Fathers, each more than two thousand years old, with Abroghia being the one we referred to as High Father. Today, 2020, they are dead. Chief repeated the phrase the same way, still looking out the window. One of my brothers must have said that in his hearing, but how could it matter?

Chief and I sat across from each other in the stretch limo and I kicked both legs out to the center to slump downward in the soft leather. Draping my arms across the back of the bench seat, I watched his profile. I know enough about human behavior to realize when a man mumbles in that fashion, he's not seeking a query. He was drunk and repeating an odd phrase that for some reason stuck in his head.

"I'd kill the Rabbit if I ever saw her," he said in the same voice, but this time as he reached the word "saw" he turned his face to mine. "I'd kill the Rabbit," he said again, now seeking my response. "Does that mean anything to you?"

I didn't reply, but watched his eyes, vainly trying to divine his thoughts on the matter. Why would he ask such an ignorant question unless the phrase meant something to him? I had my reply.

"What does it mean to you?" I ask, eyebrows up, as innocent as a lamb.

Chief exhaled a long breath and shrugged, end of topic. He looked back out the window. "Your friends were sure different."

I chuckled but he didn't turn. "Tell me about it," I said agreeing.

"I needed a Babblefish in my ear." Chief was leaning on the right side of the car and he swiveled his chin, his body still sideways. "The more they drank, the more they spoke in that top-secret language of yours." He said the last part with humor and shimmied his body to a more upright position. Out the windshield, I saw the hotel sign; we were pulling up.

"We speak at least four languages, my brothers and I," I said and closed my mouth. What the shit? I was comfortable, a little floaty from the booze, but I had spoken too close to the line. I tried to cover it with a follow-up. "How about you, Chief? Your resume said you speak English and Spanish. Any other linguistics in your lineup?"

"Does pig-Latin count?" he asked with a grin.

The limousine stopped and the driver's shape approached the tinted window. Chief exited first and I followed, neither speaking until we had hit the lobby elevator bank.

I hit our floor and the car started up before Chief said with a new smile, "You tired?"

I grinned with interest. "What do you have in mind?"

Chief nodded and when the door opened, he walked out, a little come-hear-finger wiggling over his shoulder as he left. I followed, still smiling and wondering what he was thinking. Nothing that transpired the past thirty minutes was the least bit sexual, so I worked every other possible angle. Had it to do with languages? Killing Rabbits? High Fathers? When we reached our pair of rooms, he opened his door and led me inside.

The automatic light illuminated the space in a soft amber glow, set previously by Chief I imagine. I had set mine to the same level—it comforted the eyes while providing enough to read by.

"Have a seat," he said with a knuckle to the long hotel couch. I was game and dropped into it longways, propping my feet on the other end as he disappeared into the bedroom. He returned almost immediately with a book and he dropped it in my lap as he passed to sit in the adjacent matching chair.

The Rabbit, by Beth Rider-Stone. *Shit.* Do Jersey's readers know what that is? In short, it's a book about what happened to a woman named Beth Rider when she was marked as a Rabbit by

Master Dawn. I was not involved in that fuck-up, but I read the book. Maybe this is where I admit, like the Rabbit, I believe in the Maker.

At any rate, back to Chief handing me this novel. You'd be surprised at my reaction. I forced a languid gaze and played dumb. "You want me to read this?"

"That's what they were talking about," he said making himself comfortable. He crossed one ankle over his knee, elbows on the armrests, his hands loose in his lap. He tilted his chin right as he watched for my reaction. It was a good look for him, authoritative, in charge, cocksure. I remembered my F-list.

"They? My brothers?" I asked and might have flinched. Mortals don't talk like that unless they're in a cult. He showed a grin that said, *ah-hah!*. I still played dumb, no longer tipsy and wanting to be.

"You don't want to talk about it?" he asked with another vague gesture to the book in my hand.

"I'm not in this book," I said teasing and tossed it to him eight feet away. "Say what's on your mind." He sat up enough that it dawned on me we were going to talk for hours. There'd be no fucking and I was deciding if that worked for me.

"I think this book is true and you and all those men tonight are part of this secret race of vampires." Chief did not crack a smile even though his words must have sounded strange to his own ears. Humans don't believe in vampires, why would he think the book is true? I asked him and he said, "if one plus one is two, it's true whether I believe it or not."

I pursed my lips and watched his eyes. He did not waver. He wasn't as big as I am but held his ground at every eye-meet. He had since we met. I looked to the side and said in a commanding voice, "bring every bottle of booze you have in that minibar."

Chief offered a victorious wink and rose to comply. He returned with eleven minis carried in his newly un-tucked dress shirt. He allowed them to drop across my lap and I watched the three inches of his fuzzy belly until he stepped away. He returned to his chair but with both hands, yanked the heavy furniture closer so we were half the distance apart. I remained reclined across the sofa and tossed him a Svedka.

"I'm not admitting anything, but I'll turn anything into a drinking game." I grabbed my own mini and held it up, sealed. "If you ask a question, you down a mini. Same for me. Answers can be true or false, but must be coherent. When the booze is gone, the game is done."

Chief grinned and lifted his upper body to peek in my lap. "Someone gets an extra question."

I waggled my eyebrows. "That's part of the fun."

"I'll go first," he said and gurgled down his vodka. I chuckled when he choked on the final drop. "Went down the wrong pipe," he managed and cleared his throat several times with hilarious facial expression until he could speak again. "Okay... you can lie so let me make it a good one..."

He had specific questions. What was happening? I hadn't revealed myself to any of them since Last Assembly. I wasn't about to do so with this fantastic new CEO who would serve to bring me more money than ever. While he worked his questions into the proper form, I prepared my cult responses and told myself they were all lies. I did not want the man to go away thinking the owner of Pebb Construction spent three centuries as a vampire.

"Okay, boss-man," he said with snark, a watery sparkle in his deep blue eyes after the quick shot, "You said you aren't in this book, which means you recognize it, so my question is, explain to me why you said you aren't in it."

I smiled—he worked hard to formulate a question that yes or no wouldn't serve. Plus, there was a little mind-fuck going on between us. He was leaning further forward now, leaning over his knees, and I read something hungry in his eye. Not for sex, but something... Part of my mind worked that issue while I began my answer.

"I read that book two years ago when recommended by a colleague. I recognized your Rabbit and High Father phrases from the novel when we were in the car. When we discussed it later, I felt like being a little roguish, pretending I was part of another race." I held his gaze the entire time and slowly sat up to match his posture, leaning forward over my knees with my hands dangling. I'm five inches taller and at least seventy pounds heavier, but we must have looked like a nice pair, facing off like that. "I mean, I have the look. I could be a vampire, right?"

Chief almost answered and smiled. "Is that your question?"

"Is that your second question?" I said with cheek.

"Only if that's yours."

He was quick-minded. I rolled in my bottom lip and held it with my teeth, watching his eyes still. His gaze flit to my mouth and my chin and lower before he looked back. He was straight, but I'm very beautiful. With my teeth I unscrewed my mini and downed it holding his attention. "That's my question. I know I look like one of those wraiths in the book. Am I beautiful? What does my CEO think? Go ahead."

He remained forward but blushed as the moments passed. He smiled to the side. "I can lie, remember?" I nodded. "Boss-man," he repeated and I snickered, "you look like a vampire, all right. You look like a devil. I'm fifty years old, dedicated to my children and my career, I go to church on the holidays and pray when I'm in trouble, but you get me alone and shit. I could forget myself around you. I think you're not human. Or you used to be something else. If this book is true, you could be a fallen angel in the flesh. Shit." He laughed and prepared another mini to shoot. "Satisfied?" he asked, the bottle poised by his lips.

I gave him a slow nod and he knocked it back. In five seconds, he exhaled and pound his sternum once. "Ooh, I should stick to beer." I waited for him to ask something, floating on his compliments. They had been vague, but he meant them. When he parted his lips to speak, I made a big show of opening my shirt half-way down. I don't shave my chest anymore and he laughed when I stroked over my own pecs.

"Your question?" I said with a flat expression.

"Your brothers," he said in finger quotes, "don't look like you. They're all fine-looking guys, but you look like a sex doll." He laughed at his own words. "I discern—and maybe it's the vodka speaking—but I discern you might have been an expert in seduction when you lived the old way."

"The old way," I repeated. He was too close to knowing the truth, but I was lying, right? In the morning, we would both pretend the entire thing was a game. Right? "Is that the question?" I asked and got to my feet. I took one step nearer and he leaned back, craning his face to mine. "In this pretend world of vampires and Rabbits and High Fathers, was your new boss a Sexpert?" I asked with a grin and licked my lips in slow motion. He had said he could forget himself. Had I heard that right?

"Is it pretend?" he asked in a softer, cautious voice. I took another step near, now an arm's length away and as he was seated his chin was at my belt-level.

"Everything is pretend when you're away from home, drinking with a god at 2 AM," I replied in my bedroom voice. Without planning to, I had fallen into seduction mode. The poor guy. He didn't have a chance.

"Ah-hah," he said weakly. "That's what they said in the book. They all believed they were gods until they met the real God…"

He remained seated, looking up at me, and I moved a careful palm to his cheek. He hadn't shaved since the night before and I feathered my hand across the new growth. "Whose turn is it?" I asked in a whisper meant to send chills to his flesh and it worked.

"Yours," he said, only moving his lips. I reached for a mini he held in his hand and for that two seconds, our faces were inches apart. I made certain to meet his eye up close and then stood. I sucked it down, wiped my chin with an exaggerated movement, and tossed the plastic container over my shoulder. I bent enough

to grasp his right bicep and tugged until he gained his feet. I didn't need Rakum hearing to know his heart pounded when he stood facing me, less than two feet from chest to chest.

"My question goes like this," I said very softly and watching his mouth. *"Have you ever kissed a god?"*

Chief hadn't kissed a god, hadn't kissed a man. He hadn't wanted to. White-bread, All-American, Muscular Judeo-Christian life, he didn't take drugs or abuse women. He didn't watch porn and hadn't stolen anything more than a pack of gum. But I tell you right now, dear reader, he was aching to kiss the fix-it man.

This is where my expertise comes in. He had no words and I don't know what he would have said if I didn't do my part next. I cupped his face with my palms and Chief's body responded on its own—no need for human labels of gay or bi or straight. At that instant, we were compatible, and I lowered to touch our lips. He did not return anything as I molded my mouth to his, gentle, quiet, allowing our breath to intermingle. He received me, but not fully. Not yet. I moved my palms to his neck, cradling the base of his skull. I'm huge and when a person feels my size on them, they dissolve. Chief was alpha, but he was also human. A sexual being lived inside the CEO and when three long seconds passed, our mouths touching and my hands so gentle around his head, he exhaled, and I moved in.

I'll save you the details (tick-tock, right, Jerz?), but once our tongues were dancing, two beautiful men began to undress. When I got him to the bed, he hadn't explored my body, rather he encompassed my forearms with his fingers. We were down to our boxers, kissing deeper and both aroused, and I had him sit on the edge of the bed. My eyes drank in his every inch, but he only stared at my face. This was new to me. Even straight men, when seduced by the fix-it man, mimic what is performed on their person. Chief didn't reach out. His eyes flicked down when I slid off my final garment, but he hadn't yet volunteered contact. When I reached for his hand to place it on my chest, he held it there unmoving, looking into my face. Part of him was petrified but an equal part was already fucking a man for the first time. Another long moment passed with his palm encompassing my right breast, in place but not moving, and I made up my mind.

One gentle push to his shoulder and he lay back, looking up at me as if I was a giant and he was a child. Completely out of character, I whispered, "Do you want me to leave?"

"No," he croaked and said more firmly, "No. Lie down." I gave him a small grin and lay alongside. I started the show and he said in my ear very small, *The Puppeteer is watching..."*

I nodded without breaking stride in my duties.

[Fuck, Jerz, tell your readers, Darcy Vandiver knows the Maker. I trust Him. I'm getting to understand Him. And shit, I'm a work in progress, always will be.]

I told Chief to shut-it and he said nothing else. The CEO and the Boss-man wrestled until they fell asleep, in the same bed like an old married couple. In the morning, Chief left as I showered. He took a cab to the airport and hired a new flight. He left me a note, which I'll share here by permission.

Boss-man, I enjoyed our bonding adventure, and I look forward to bringing Pebb Construction to higher and higher levels over the next several quarters. Maybe I'll see you at the Christmas Party in Cancun. Bam-bam said it is always a huge hit and drinking games are encouraged. Kazak! ~ (name redacted)

So, there you go. Chief is still my CEO and I will seek him out at the party. I always have plenty of minis in my luggage.

~ D. Vandiver

Jersey's Parting Words

So, there you have it, my rebuttal.

A couple of years have passed since I wrote the preface and I've met the Rabbit, Beth Rider and Rakum-turned-human Michael Stone (who turned out to be okay). Read her series, as it describes in detail my beautiful lost race. Read the next few pages to get a taste of her writing. I hope you remember Jersey and Darcy. **We are much more than side characters.**

Visit me at www.emiljersey.com. And **I'm writing again,** this time about a brother (based on a true story) who didn't take the transformation too well. He became a killer and his Rakum companion convinces him to see a therapist (who has issues of her

own and becomes entangled with his psychosis). It'll be good stuff, and of course, sexy. Like me.

And Darcy's sexy memoir is out. Go to my website or search me on Amazon for all my work. I'm writing for you.

Jersey

Emil Jersey, Athens, GA 2019

Novel Excerpt

Rabbit: Chasing Beth Rider
Book One of the Rabbit Saga
Ellen C Maze
13+, L S V
99 cents on Kindle
(Paperback price varies.)

❖ Don't Bother to Scream

Author Beth Rider left the room dark and collapsed face down on the hotel bed. She had no energy to even turn on a lamp. She'd spent the last two days and most of both evenings in various bookstores signing novels for her readers. Her left hand was numb from the effort, but for the most part, each book signing had been a joy. Only the dark maniac at the Buckhead BooksAMillion left a sour taste in her mouth. *"Watch your back!"* he had hissed, and she had thought she heard it in her mind, as in telepathically. But how did that make sense? She had put him out of her mind, but now, she shivered as she recalled the hellish encounter.

Beth flipped onto her back, still lying long-ways across the king-sized bed. A furtive movement to her right, beyond the glow of the tiny nightlight caught her attention and she sat up. She was not alone.

"Is this the way you watch your back?" a husky whisper rasped. Beth jumped to her feet and lunged for the door. Before she could take three steps, the dark form across the room grabbed her from behind. "Don't bother to scream…"

As one steel-like arm wrapped uncomfortably about her chest holding her immobile, the other hand covered her mouth. Beth could not see her attacker, but it was definitely the tattooed monster from the night before. Beth prayed in her heart for help and went limp in her attacker's grasp.

"You're quite the nuisance. Have you any idea the trouble you're causing my people?" The voice paused and then continued in a guttural chortle that chilled Beth's soul. "I could handle this so many ways, Miss Rider. So many ways…"

Beth squeezed her eyes closed, unable to fathom the meaning of his accusation.

"Bel suggested I snuff you out, right here, right now." The stranger waited briefly for a response, but then continued his one-way conversation in a gleeful tone. "But Tomás, on the other hand... his idea intrigues me. Want to know what Elder Tomás suggested?"

Beth did not respond, still praying for divine rescue.

"He said you'd make a delightful Rabbit." The giant smacked his lips. "Hah! I haven't marked a Rabbit since… *damn*… it's been a long time. Would you rather die now or become a Rabbit for my pups to play with?"

Beth didn't attempt to answer, even though the thought was moot with her mouth covered. She opened her eyes and trained them on the outline of the curtained window across the dark room.

"I'll tell you," the man continued in a teaching tone, as if she had asked a question. "A Rabbit is a toy for my pups. You know, a papa wolf finds a rabbit, marks it with his scent, turns it over to his pups, and they play with it. They practice their technique on it. They attack it again and again until it's worn out, or insane, or both."

The man paused and Beth worked to ignore the rising panic in her gut. Somehow, she knew he was not going to end her life, but whatever he had in mind was going to be horrible.

"Most of the time, Rabbits give up *long* before we're done with 'em. I wonder how long you'll last? I wonder how many of my pups you can entertain before you kill yourself?" The man's tone turned wistful as he finished his thought. Still with his left arm around her from behind and that hand pressed firmly over her mouth, his right arm disappeared and she felt his fingers against her throat.

"Now, hush, this might sting a bit…" His fingernail pressed into the curve of Beth's neck and continue inward until the skin split and blood trickled out of the small wound. "Are you the quiet type, little Rabbit?" He encircled the wound with his lips, his tongue pressing against her skin.

Not even aware that she was going to do so, Beth leapt into action. With mighty effort, she pushed off with all of the strength she could muster. Although she didn't break free, the man's lips slipped away and she grunted with victory. As she struggled to free herself from the death grip on her face, the man secured her once more with his strong right arm. His left hand shifted slightly and now covered her mouth *and* her nose.

"Can you wriggle free from this, you brat?"

Beth increased her attempts to break loose; she couldn't breathe and as panic crept in, all of her internal prayers ceased.

"I'm gonna mark you now. It'll only take a minute if you're still."

Beth continued to strain, all of her senses on alert. She was no longer a rational being, but rather a wild animal fighting for her life. Just as she thought she might lose consciousness, the man's hand slipped off her nose and she took in a painful breath. The man shuffled her to the bed and forced her into a lying position, his looming shape taking a straddling stance over her. Beth's eyes grew wide in the dim room and she thrashed wildly.

"Be still, you shit," the monster hissed and again, closed her airway with a slight movement of his hand. His weight over her abdomen caused enormous pressure to her diaphragm and Beth grew still.

"Move again, I beg you," the man rasped. "I don't like you enough to explore what else you might be good for."

Horrified at his sexual threat, Beth quieted every muscle.

"That's right, heheh," he chuckled, his putrid breath falling on her cheeks. "You're too school-teacher for me, but I have *lotsa* brothers." The monster leaned down to sniff her hairline. "*Yeahhhh,* I can think of three or four who like them clean and innocent..."

"Mmmm!" Beth mumbled into his hand, her eyes vainly seeking his in the dim light.

"My mark will change you, make you smell like me, and then *all* of my pups will like you—*a lot.*" He stressed the last two words and held her gaze. "I am about to uncover your mouth. Hush, submit, and this will be over quickly. Understand?"

Beth nodded, her eyes bulging with terror. She didn't know what he intended to do, but he said it would be quick. Beth held on to that assurance and closed her eyes. The man's clammy hand slipped from her mouth and a warm liquid touched her tongue and rapidly filled her mouth.

"I hope you're a swallower, Miss Rider," her gruff attacker jibed and pinched closed her nostrils. "All of it. *Swallow.*"

Beth's mind flashed to her novels. Her characters were forced to drink blood. Did this lunatic think he was a vampire? Is that what the entire ordeal was about? A psychotic and deluded fan of her novels acting out his fantasies? Even as her mind raced with comparisons, Beth swallowed to keep from choking. Immediately, the man removed his hands from her face and placed them down on the pillow to either side of her head. He looked upon her and now his fetid breath fell on her forehead.

"Wait for it..." the dark giant whispered.

He was waiting for something to happen and Beth opened her eyes to meet his glittering gaze. In the darkness, she saw only the reflection of the nightlight in her attacker's reddened eyes. Focusing on the man's scar, Beth worked to regain her composure. *What now?* Her mind was clearing, her morbid fear passing... What was he waiting for? Precisely five seconds later, Beth's stomach turned inside out.

"Ugghhhhh!" she groaned, writhing in pain beneath her monstrous enemy. The man did not cover her mouth as she twisted and strained beneath him, every nerve afire.

"Shiiiiiit..." he chuckled, "that looks painful."

Beth made an attempt to conceal her discomfort, and soon, the acid burn in her middle subsided. As she settled her frightened but angry gaze into that of her attacker, her pain melted into nausea and then was gone altogether.

"You're hilarious," he said, spittle falling on her face. Beth didn't respond and the dark brute sat up, still holding his bulk up just enough to prevent crushing her. His right hand lifted and dropped to her shirt, dragging heavily across her breasts. *"Ehhhh, so tender; my pups are going to be thanking me forever,"* he muttered. With one last lewd pass, he put both palms to his thighs and looked upon her. "Do you have any idea what just happened?"

Beth only glared, unsure if she could control her tongue if she spoke.

"Mad little bunny," the man chuckled and patted the top of her head. "My mark is on you and that makes you a Rabbit. Now, I am releasing you into the world so my pups can hunt you down. No matter where you go, they'll seek you out. Did you know that a wolf can sniff out a rabbit from as far away as a mile? My pups' senses are far greater than that and you will smell like steak roasting on an outdoor grill. You know how wonderful that smells? *Mmmmm."*

He paused for Beth to respond, but again she refused.

"All of my brethren will want a shot at you. A juicy new Rabbit is a rarity they will exploit to the max and in every way imaginable."

As numbness seeped up her spinal cord, Beth realized she was losing consciousness. She watched the silhouette of the big man as he crawled away and then stood.

"Let's see...where is it?"

He reached for her purse on the nightstand. Through heavy eyelids, she watched him locate her wallet and pluck out a plastic card that glinted in the low light. Beth whimpered as he dropped the purse beside her, her driver's license in his possession. Beth's head swam. She was done fighting, but the monster spoke again and she made an attempt to comprehend.

"I like to know where my Rabbits are headed. Montgomery, Alabama? I have some pups *'round them parts*." He spoke the last few words in a put-on Southern accent. "They haven't seen a Rabbit in a *long* time," he laughed to himself with a shake of the head. "My favorite lieutenant's in Montgomery; he'll find you first. You won't like him; he's horny and hungry *all the time.*"

Chuckling, the man backed toward the door and wiggled his fingers in Beth's direction.

"Sleep now, Rabbit. But tomorrow..." He opened the door to the hallway. "You better start running." And he was gone.

Beth tried to thank God she was alive, but numbness overtook her brain and she slipped away, falling into a deep sleep. In her dreams, she was running and staying out of reach of the wolves.

Just barely.

❖ **Nip It in the Bud**

Jack Dawn shoved Kite to the ground and beat his chest like a gorilla. He'd never been bested, not in twelve hundred years; no way this feeble pup was going to get the better of him tonight. Jack feigned toward him and the kid winced. It was good to be the king.

He'd begun his evening at a local brothel with a few of his brothers and now they were winding down, enjoying their nightly ritual of pounding each other until they collapsed or cried uncle. Kite endured a special beat-down for something he'd said over a month ago. There was no need to remind him of his error; it was more fun to slap the snot out of him and watch his eyes grow wide with fear. It would make the kid stronger. Jack was slapped around plenty when he was young and he recalled every excruciating millisecond.

"So, what about that Rabbit you marked?" Elder Tomás spoke with a thick Spanish accent, watching from a few feet away.

"What's to say?" Jack booted Kite in the shoulder to hear him yelp. When the kid fell silent, he turned to Tomás. "Well?"

"There's a whisper going around that Stone isn't playing fair."

"Don't you know better than to listen to gossip?" Jack approached his friend and punched his shoulder. Not quite as tall as Jack, but nearly as muscular, Tomás braced himself, effectively nullifying the jab.

"It's not gossip, Brother. Tyson said—"

"Tyson? That miserable waste of space? Come on, Tomás. Shut up about Tyson!" Jack growled and threatened the other Elder with a raised fist.

Tomás stepped forward and bared his teeth, wrapping strong fingers around Jack's closed hand. Jack pushed against him and soon added his upper body strength, leaning in to press through. Tomás matched his great physical might perfectly. As they tested each other, Tomás spat his next words into Jack's sweating face.

"Stone's gone soft," he grunted with effort. "Let's go down to Montgomery and check it out." Tomás clocked Jack under the chin. "If Stone's behaving, no problem. But if he's—"

Jack returned Tomás's uppercut with a powerful double blow to the kidney. Tomás crumpled to the ground but didn't cry out. He remained on the carpet, drew up his knees, and caught his breath.

"Behaving? That's my *lieutenant,* you asshole!" Jack kicked the Elder's nearest shin hard.

Tomás made no notice of the blow. "If he's gone soft," he said in a forced whisper, "you're gonna want to nip that in the bud."

Jack frowned. "Seriously, what does Tyson know?"

"It's not Tyson alone." Tomás put out his hand and Jack pulled him to his feet. "Others sense the same thing. Don't you? He's *your* favored one—surely you've read his intentions," Tomás said and raised his fists, pugilist style.

Jack ignored the offer and turned, leaving the large room he'd modified especially for roughhousing. When he entered the kitchen, Tomás was right behind him, followed by a very bloody Kite. Behind him, entered Beryl, one of a set of twins Jack was discipling.

"What about it?" Tomás pressed as he pulled a beer from the fridge. He tossed the can to Jack who caught it without looking up.

"I got this. *Shit!* End of discussion." Jack popped open the can and drank the entire contents without pause. He tossed the empty to Beryl who dropped it into the trash. "I should have killed that woman and been done with it. Why do I always listen to you?"

"Blame yourself for lovin' me so much." Tomás smiled and then his eyes narrowed. "Did you hear Kilmeade's report?"

"Kilmeade..." Jack growled the name. Younger by centuries, Elder Kilmeade suffered under the delusion that he was greater than Jack. No Elder alive could realistically claim such a thing and merely looking upon the arrogant ass's face was infuriating. So, when the Elder sent out his latest Rabbit report, Jack had ignored it.

Observing Jack's surface thoughts, Tomás shook his head. "You should have listened. He's pompous, but he watches out for the Brethren."

"You can suck him off later, asshole. What did he say?"

"Maybe I will," Tomás chuckled. "He's more my type than your ugly ass..."

"What did he say?" Jack grumbled with a frown, his hand going to the deep scar over his cheek. He loved his face; if Tomás didn't, that was on him. *He* was the one always coming around. Tomás saw what he'd been thinking.

"Come here, precious," he cooed and reached for Jack's thick neck. Jack shoved him backward with more power than necessary and the brother hit the tiled floor, knocking into a daydreaming Kite on the way down.

"What did he say?!" Jack bellowed, leaning over his friend with a boot poised to stomp his middle. Tomás laughed and showed his palms.

"Our beautiful brother Kilmeade reported that he overheard two grunts planning to run away." He waited for Jack's expression to lose the irritation and reflect the seriousness of the situation.

"Overheard?" Jack asked and put out his hand to help Tomás stand. "Or read?"

Tomás tipped his chin. "Overheard—you know he hears better than any of us."

"SHIT, Tomás. Finish up!" Jack shouted and angrily sought Kite who stood to the side. With a sudden roundhouse kick, he sent the kid sprawling to the floor and met the other Elder's eye. "What did the wonderful and amazing Kilmeade say? Please, tell me."

Tomás grinned, obviously pleased he provoked Jack to such an extent. "Two of Emil's pups were plotting an escape. They spouted some religious shit and dropped off his radar."

Jack narrowed his eyes. "Dropped off?"

"Disappeared. Line severed." Tomás rubbed his face. "Hell, two of Bel's pups disappeared just tonight. And he described the same thing—the tether was gone. As if they blinked out of existence. That makes twenty Rakum so far that we know of."

Jack cursed and hit the wall with a closed fist. Powdered plaster filtered down from the ceiling onto his bald head. "This is *ridiculous*. Stone's a monster."

"His line still up?" Tomás asked, eyebrows raised.

Jack peeked inside and sought Stone's mental link. "He's there. No change. But twenty brethren? Has that woman unleashed some sort of disease on us? On my lieutenant?"

Tomás commiserated, his fists to his hips. "How are we to know? Thousands of years and nothing like this has ever happened. Should we request a meeting with the Fathers?"

Beryl cleared his throat and since he was an inferior, Jack sent him a glare. Not yet commissioned, over the past few years Beryl had earned his way into Jack's inner circle. When he sent Michael Stone to Montgomery, he moved Beryl and his identical twin brother, Meryl, right under him, intending to promote them to captain as soon as they had a few more years under their belts. Young, passionate, and impetuous, the boys performed as two bodies with one magnificent brain, and it was no use to separate them for long.

Tonight, Meryl was taking care of a mission for Jack across town and Beryl stayed behind. He liked to have one of them around at all times. He liked to watch them work. And he liked to watch them, *period*. Identical in every way, the boys had wavy brown hair and fawn-hazel eyes that mesmerized mortal and Rakum alike. The brotherhood considered the boys' appearance unmatched in their generation, with perfect facial symmetry, skin the color of creamy coffee, and a killer smile, and both with the disposition of their seed donor, the mighty Father Umbarto—also Jack's natural father. Ninety-nine Elders wanted them and Jack didn't share, never had and he never would.

Jack grinned inwardly as all this ran past his mind. As a fantastic telepath himself, Beryl appeared to have read him, a tiny sparkle in his eye as he prepared to explain his uncharacteristic interruption.

"You got something to add, B?" Jack asked, knowing his normally terse tone inevitably lifted when he addressed the twins.

Beryl carefully chose his words and in a voice as smooth as silk, he said, "Father Abroghia once told a story." He paused and met the eyes of each man. "Two thousand years ago, many Rakum fell away, grabbing onto a new religion circling the planet at that time. Abroghia was there."

Jack considered the tale. Abroghia was the only Father that went back that far. The other nine were old, no doubt, but Abroghia had seen at least two millennia and was widely respected as the ultimate leader of their Race. He nodded at the boy who returned a tight smile. It was the closest thing to affection that they had between them and it suited them both.

"Could be it's coming around again," Tomás interjected. "Twenty of the brethren gone underground. Hiding from us. Hiding from *you.*" Tomás headed out of the kitchen. "You need to go to Montgomery and eliminate that Rabbit. Hell, I'll go with you. It'll be fun."

Jack watched him go and then glared at Kite who stepped back, as if awaking from a trance, his marbles scrambled.

"We'll leave at sundown," Jack called to Tomás and then reached for Kite's upper arm. The boy knew better than to evade him and he stood under Jack's hard gaze suppressing a shudder. Jack eyed Beryl and he stepped behind the younger Rakum to wrap his arms firmly around his chest. Kite closed his eyes and pressed his lips together. It stunk being least in the kingdom.

END EXCERPT

Blood, Sex & Violence A Vampire's Rebuttal is a spin-off novel of Rabbit: Chasing Beth Rider, written by Ellen C. Maze.

In 2020, watch for Emil Jersey's second novel, MALCONTENT, about what happened to one of his brothers who went insane after 11/13. Sign up for email alerts at www.emiljersey.com

JOIN THE CHASE
Rabbit: Chasing Beth Rider by Ellen C. Maze
#1 Top-Rated in Horror/Occult by Amazon Readers
Visit the author at www.ellencmaze.com
Twitter: @authorellenmaze
Visit the publisher at www.littleronipublishers.com /Run-Rabbit-Books.php

---

[i] *Conundrum: The Lost Rabbit*, by Ellen C. Maze, Little Roni Publishers, DUE TO PUBLISH WINTER 2019. Follow Author Ellen C Maze on Amazon for release updates, or on www.ellencmaze.com.

www.ingramcontent.com/pod-product-compliance
Lightning Source LLC
Chambersburg PA
CBHW070847120626
46556CB00002B/908

"Instant Chemistry Series"

Running

Into

You

Taylor Love

Taylor Made Day Dreams
Bringing an "imaginative break" to your day!

Running Into You
Copyright © 2018 Taylor Love

This is a work of fiction. Names, characters, places and incidents are either the product of the author's imagination or are used fictitiously, and any resemblance to actual persons, living or dead, business establishments, events or locales is entirely coincidental.

To the extent that the image or images on the cover of this book depict a person or persons, such person or persons are merely models. This book is for adult readership and may contain adult situations, language and sexual content.

ISBN 978-1-948383-00-4

Taylor Made Daydreams
P.O Box 85458
Westland, MI 48185
www.TaylorMadeDaydreams.com